MARY JANE'S WAR

A Civil War Novel
Based on a True Story

Mary Jane's husband died from a wound received in the battle of New Market during the Civil War. She took a pair of mules and a wagon 120 miles through the mountains and enemy lines during the winter of 1865 to pick up her husband's remains to bring them back home to Monroe County for burial.

Mary Jane's War
A Civil War Novel
Based on a True Story

Joe B. Roles—2002
7450 Adams Park Ct.
Annandale, VA 22003
joeroles@aol.com
703.304.6100
2nd edition 2010

This is a work of fiction because the facts are very
limited, all the characters and events portrayed in
this novel are used fictitiously.

DEDICATION

Malcolm McKinley Weikle
1925 — 2002

Malcolm was born and raised in Lillydale, West Virginia and has been a local historian of Lillydale for many years. He perpetuated the story of Mary Jane for years.

He was a mathematics teacher in Ohio. Malcolm once said that he worked and slept in Ohio, but lived in Lillydale.

BACKGROUND NOTES

Notes for the reader to better understand the book.

- The town of Centerville is now Greenville, WV.

- Up the Valley of Virginia is toward Roanoke and down the Valley is toward Winchester.

- Red Sweets Spring is now Sweet Chalybeate Springs.

- Monroe County separated from Greenbrier County in 1799.

- Monroe and Greenbrier Counties was part of Virginia until June 15, 1862 then they became part of the new state of West Virginia.

- The town of Union is the County seat of Monroe County.

- The Virginia Central Railroad became the Chesapeake and Ohio RR and now is CSX RR.

- Dinner was the noon meal and supper the evening meal.

- Washington College is now Washington and Lee University.

- The Kountz House was disassembled and moved a second time to the Knobs and the bloody footprint is now on a bedroom ceiling.

CHAPTER ONE

Lillydale

1836

It was the middle of summer and Mary Jane Arnott loved to walk to the Post Office at Salt Sulphur Springs in Virginia and did so every chance she had. With all the men and boys working in the farm fields and her stepmother caring for her new baby, Caroline, the Post Office chore was Mary Jane's.

Mary Jane had turned eleven just two months ago. Everything outside of her home excited her, the neighbors, visiting the general store and watching the growing summer resort at Salt Sulphur Springs, especially all the strange people who came to spend the winter there. Her father's uncle, Jessie Arnott had built the stone bath house there twenty years ago. Then the hotel was built a year later and as the resorts popularity grew it attracted more and more guests each summer.

The three-mile stretch from her home in Lillydale to "The Salt" was tiring but fun. It gave Mary Jane time to be alone, away from her siblings, time to think, dream and see the outside world. Even though the sun was at its peak but the cool mountain air made the walk delightful. She would have loved an early morning walk, but her father would never let her leave home until all the morning chores...... were completed and she had to return in time to begin preparing the supper. With six miles ahead of her to walk back and forth, she didn't have a lot of free time to play.

No one had seen a buffalo in the county since she was born, but panthers, black bears and wolves a-plenty roamed free. They normally wouldn't attack in the heart of the day, but she still carried a five-foot long, pointed stick made of oak, for her protection.

Her older brothers taught her how to use the stick in the event that a panther or mountain lion should attack. If a panther should jump toward her, she would place the butt of the pole on the ground and point the sharp end toward the panther over her head. If the animal came at her low and head-on, she was to aim the point at its mouth or eyes. Never try to run away, they said, as it would expose her back to an attack. A couple times as she walked, she had heard a rustle in the leaves that seemed to keep pace with her, but she hadn't actually seen anything in the middle of the day.

About a mile along the way, she came upon the Baker home place. If Mrs. Frederick Baker Sr. saw Mary Jane coming she would always come out to see her and inquire about Mary Jane's Grand-father and Grandmother, Mr. and Mrs. Henry Arnott Sr. Their family had both come from Germany and eventually settled at Lil-lydale about the same time. The families had always been close; they walked to church together and spent many Sundays visiting.

Mrs. Baker would offer her a cup of spring water and a piece of blackberry pie, which Mary Jane seldom refused. They would talk "a spell" and Mary Jane would be on her way as she was always in a hurry to get to The Salt to see what was going on there.

She passed the Pyles home place and waved. A little farther up the road she walked past the Weikle place on the right. The house and garden were near the road and the Weikle children were out weeding the garden. Ten-year-old "Wild" Weikle let fly with a green tomato that went past just over her head. She laughed and he flung another one that missed its mark, which just riled him up. At that Wild picked a big ripe tomato and that spattered just in front of her. Mrs. Weikle stepped out the door and declared,

"It's a sin to waste the food that God has given us"

Then she grabbed a switch and set out to do God's work.

For the most part the road was good and had been shaled this past spring by the neighbors who used the road. She soon came to the section of the road that was steep, descending down to The Salt. She could see the church and the store were near Pepper Run, a small cold-water stream that fed into Indian Creek from "The Knobs" at the resort.

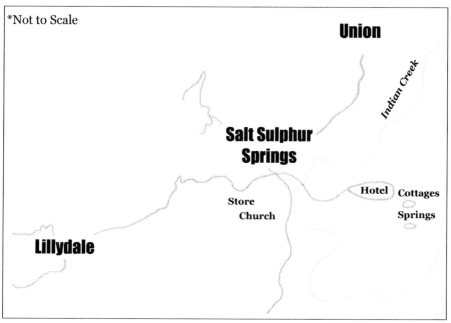

The church and the store, both about ten years old, were built of limestone. It was the first stone church she had ever seen and it looked magnificent with its tall columns and high steeple. They say the Episcopalians from South Carolina, who had come to the resort to spend the summer, had built it. They even brought a reverend by the name of John Johns all the way from Baltimore to preach for the summer months. It was grander than any Methodist church that her family attended.

Her grandfather told her that these two buildings were built under the supervision of Mr. Addam Foalden, now pronounced Fullen, a good man of German descent who lived a mile or so down Indian Creek below the resort.

The store building had two stories with two front porches that extended across the front of the building. The Post Office and store were on the main floor while the second floor contained four guest-rooms that were rented to the overflow of guests from the hotel.

Holding court on the store's front porch was Mr. Seldon, an older gentleman; slim with an age cleaved face, and who always wore a coat and tie. He considered himself the squire of The Salt. He was always there to advise and talk with anyone who happened by. There were always others who loafed on the porch to see what was going on across Indian Creek at the hotel. The porch was high enough to view the entrance and the bathhouses. They would just sit there watching guests come and go in their beautiful custom made coaches, pulled by four horses with the guests dressed in finery not found in these parts.

Mary Jane spoke to all on the porch, and then hurried in to get the mail. She was a shy little girl due to having cut off the first finger on her left hand at the age of ten while chopping the head of a chicken. She was afraid people would tease her about her hand.

Sure enough, her father Henry Arnott Jr. had a letter, which Mary Jane paid two cents to receive as the person receiving the mail paid for all postage at that time. Mr. Burton told her to pass the word in Lillydale that the Pyles and Ellisons also had mail. Mr. Burton liked to get all the mail out and collected so he could send the postage back to Covington with the mail driver on his next delivery, which was twice a week. Only then did the postmaster get paid.

Mary Jane then bought some baking powder and needles for her stepmother. There was also a new jar of hard candy on the counter and it wouldn't do just to buy a couple of pieces as she had nine brothers and sisters who were still at home. It was either one for everybody or none so she decided to pass on it.

Back on the porch she paused to hear any news to take home, as she surely would be asked at suppertime that night.

Mr. Seldon had that lean, underfed look. He never married and lived with his uncle. God only knows if they did any cooking there. He had some education and the mannerisms of a gentleman, even claimed to have read the law at one time but never practiced it. In fact he never seemed to do anything except occasional trading to keep a few coins in his pocket. There was one thing that Mr. Seldon was good at and that was keeping up with the news; some people in teasing called him "Monroe County's" only newspaper.

Mr. Seldon said that the hotel was asking for some good well-fed and dressed mutton as some of the guests had acquired a taste for it when they visited England. The problem was that it was hard to raise sheep in Monroe County due to the predatory wolf population. There had been a bounty on wolves but the sheriff just announced an increase to $8.00 per head. That made it more worthwhile to hunt and trap wolves.

The Erskins Hotel on the hill above the resort rose fast as Mr. Phil Collins, Master Mason from the Valley of Virginia, had arrived to help speed up the work. He was also looking to buy a small farm down Lillydale way.

"They also have some new school books at Shanklin's store in Union," he said, "I know one of them is called 'Pike's Arithmetic'."

He explained that there were public schools in the county now but they didn't work so well. You see, the rich folks send their children to private schools and feel they shouldn't have to pay taxes for public schools. The poor people are too proud to send their children to free schools so as a result only about ten percent of the children get educated. Mr. Seldon urged Mary Jane to get her father to buy some books and get the older children to teach her.

"What's new at your house?" he asked.

She said her fifteen year-old brother Cabel Morgan Arnott was sick and not doing very well. Her father said that if he were not better by tomorrow he would call a doctor.

Mary Jane allowed that she better start home now, as it would be late afternoon by the time she got home and the family would start to fuss if she were late.

As she walked home she started to think about school. She hadn't been to school much even though she would like to go. She actually went to school for a couple months each year. Her brother, Zachariah Phillips Arnott, is a good student and her father sends him to Mr. Caldwell's Private School in Centerville. Her brother gets the first schooling and if there's money left over then the girls get some schooling.

If her grandfather, Henry Arnott Sr., had told her once he had told her a hundred times, that when he came to Lillydale this road was already here. It had been made by hoofs of buffalo that had taken the shortest route from lower Indian Creek to The Salt to lick brine around the springs. The Indians also used this trial to go get mud from the iodine spring to put on their wounds to keep down infection.

Her grandfather had taken great pleasure over the years by telling stories of his family coming to Monroe County, although it wasn't Monroe County then, it was part of Greenbrier County until 1799.

Grandfather's parents came from a place called Bavaria in Germany. The States of the Empire of Germany were at war constantly and times were difficult. King George II of England was recruiting for the colonies at the time so the Arnotts accepted passage to this country.

Henry Arnott Sr. always liked to tell that he was born March 12, 1761, in Orange County, New York. His father, William, later moved his family to Sussex County, New Jersey. There, Henry Sr. and his father William joined the 26th Battalion of the Virginia Infantry in 1776 and served with that unit until 1782 mostly in the State of New York. While in the service, he married Elizabeth Truesdale also of Sussex County, on August 15, 1780.

During the Revolutionary War he served under Captain Gordon, Major Logan and Colonel Wisenfelt along with other men from Virginia. They made Virginia sound like a wonderful place to live.

Henry Sr. always said that he would never forget that winter day in 1782 when a rider approached the camp and shouted,

"The War is over! The War is over!"

He had carried the news from General Washington that the British had surrendered in a place called Yorktown, Virginia. Oh how he would have liked to have been there!

Private Arnott along with his fellow hungry, threadbare troops gathered to lift their faces to the sky to give thanks that this plague called war is over.

As he prepared for the long walk home from Albany, New York, little did he know that his travels were just beginning.

At home it was a matter of swapping one set of hard times for another as the new nation, called The United States of America, was born into a great depression. The country was in debt, shipping had been disrupted, money was scarce and there was no market for crops or livestock. Henry Sr. struggled in New Jersey to make a living the next several years while working on a farm for a large landowner as his young family grew. There was his first child, Elizabeth, born in 1781, Martha in 1785, Deborah in 1787, William T. in 1789 and Mary Jane's Father, Henry Jr., born there in 1791.

By 1793, after an appeal to his old company commander, Captian Gordon, Henry Sr. received a land grant in Western Virginia. There he could own land of his own.

The land grant instructed him to report to the county surveyor's office in Lewisburg, Greenbrier County, Virginia. He had no idea where that was as it was not on any map of that day. He was told that it was up the Valley of Virginia.

That year of 1793, Henry Sr., age 33, his wife Elizabeth, also age 33, his five children along with a brother Jesse and his family, loaded all their belongings into a covered wagon and headed south to Philadelphia. They had no idea how far it was to western Virginia but Henry had walked and camped all over the states of New York and New Jersey and had all the confidence that he needed to make the trip.

The roads were flat near the City of Philadelphia, which had a population of 31,000 people at the time and it was an amazement to all who traveled there.

Just out of the city, the road split. One road heading west to Pittsburgh and the other to the Southwest across the Potomac River at Harper's Ferry and then up the Valley of Virginia between the Blue Ridge Mountains on the south and the Unakas Mountains on the north.

They joined up with other wagons for safety as they heard rumors of Indian attacks along the way. In the wagon trains were others of German descent headed for Greenbrier County and they were Wesleyans of the Methodist faith, which gave comfort to the Arnotts.

It took all summer long to travel from New Jersey to a place called Fincastle. From there they headed due west along the Lewis Trail that would later become the Mid-Land Trail to the Kanawha River. The trail twisted along rivers and between mountains to Lewisburg, a frontier town that had built up around Fort Lewis. By then, the rough travel and cooperation had bonded the families together and they petitioned the surveyor to give them adjoining land. The clerk, in his wisdom, saw fit to give them land, although not joining but in the same vicinity. From Lewisburg the descent down to the Greenbrier River at Ronceverte and after fording the river they traveled toward Union on a road that was little more than an Indianan trail. They ran out of daylight as they approached the plains of Pickaway.

"Oh, what beautiful country" they exclaimed.

There next day they traveled to the village of Union and then on to the salt spring two miles to the southwest.

There they rested for three days gathering food, which included wild turkeys. The men then followed a buffalo trail to land between Back Creek and Laurel Creek. They found the location as Mr. Frederick Baker Sr. lived in a cabin near there and showed the new comers where the land was located. The place was called Lillydale.

Henry Sr., back at the camp at The Salt, feasted on a smoked wild turkey leg and declared,

"What wonderful land we have! Although not large and flat as in the Valley but we have fields, as much as a man can work, with streams and mountains full of game. Best of all, it is our land!"

Just then Mary Jane was distracted from her memories by a galloping horse approaching. As it drew closer it was her older brother William and he was in a hurry. He reined up long enough to tell her that Cabel had taken a turn for the worse and that he was going to Union to fetch the doctor. He told her,

"Run on home now, they'll need you there."

As she ran the last mile home, her mind was racing. Her fifteen-year-old brother had been complaining to stomach pains for the past few days but it didn't seem serious. She wondered what could it be? By the time she reached home her grandfather and grandmother were there. They gave him buttermilk to sooth his stomach, but he had a high fever and was in pain. Mary Jane threw herself into her chores and helped to prepare dinner. She looked out to see the older members of the family attending to Cabel on the cool back porch. They had brought in cold water from the mountain spring and were applying cold rags to his feverish body.

The family took turns eating as others stayed with Cabel. Henry Jr. watched for the doctor to come. Grandmother Elizabeth was giving Cabel a few sips of Golden Seal, a cure-all, but he was drifting in and out of sleep. The family took turns at praying and singing hymns to comfort him.

As it started to get dark, Cabel was in a deep sleep and his breathing was ever so slight. Henry Jr. was walking the front porch keeping an eye on the road. He listened to the night, for drumming of hoofs and metal rims on stone. At the first sound he rushed off the porch to the road to see William on horseback and Dr. Mütter and the doctor agreed to help out a good German family.

After examining Cabel and asking the family questions, Dr. Mütter took the two Henry's aside and explained that it appeared to be a ruptured appendix and it had poised his blood and he was beyond operating on. Since Cabel was near the end, all they could do was try to comfort him, as he was not likely to last through the night. The doctor gave him a morphine medication and departed. The neighbors had seen the doctor going to the Arnott home and they were now starting to arrive. By midnight Cabel has surrendered to his illness and the family and neighbors gathered for prayer. Death and illness in one family always affected the neighbors, as they were all so close.

Mary Jane was so afraid. She hated deaths and funerals as it reminded her of her mother's death when she was just three months shy of being five years old. All she could remember was that her mother was in bed sick for a long time and that the neighbors had put a pan of water under her bed to bring down her fever.

Her mother Mary Polly Phillips Arnott had died on Saturday June 2, 1830 at the age of thirty-seven leaving a husband and nine children under the age of sixteen.

Mary Jane was undone by the confusion of the wake and all the neighbors talking. She didn't want to go to her mother's funeral as it meant that her mother was leaving. After the funeral her grandmother had taken her, her younger sister and brother Addison Washington home with her to live for a while. For weeks after she couldn't bear the thought of rain falling on her mother's grave.

Most of the family had sat up through the night with Cabel. After breakfast, the neighbors came with baskets of food and prepared to relieve the family so they could rest.

The men of the community organized the burial. They had to work fast as it was summer and the days were warming up. By mid-morning the chores were assigned. Digging the grave was a sacred act and assigned to three close family friends: Mr. Fredrick Baker, Mr. George Weikle and Mr. Frances Ellison. Mr. Fisher and his son were assigned the task of making the coffin and marker.

But the most pressing task at hand was preparing the body, as there was no way of preserving it. It had been moved to the side of the porch shaded by a large sycamore tree. They had to dress the body before it became stiff, for it will swell once it becomes stiff, then it is hard to do anything with it. One elderly lady claimed that she could hear bones in the arms and legs break as the body swells. This upset his brothers and sisters to no end. One lady laid a rag that had been soaked in soda water over his face while another looked for silver coins to lay on his eyes to keep them closed. Had they been copper coins they would have turned the skin green. If you bury someone with their eyes open, you could see the devil in his eyes fighting the soul.

Once the body was dressed it was hauled to and placed in a cave along Laurel Creek to keep it cool. Henry Sr. had sent for the Preacher in Centreville but he couldn't come until tomorrow as he was out visiting the "shut-in" members of his church and wouldn't be home until late.

By afternoon, the grave detail had finished their tasks and had gone home to clean up for the wake that night. The casket had been built from some sawed poplar that Henry Jr. had been storing in his barn and they were a wreath of holly and cedar as well as sprays of hemlock for the burial service.

It was late afternoon and everything had been done except for one important chore which was usually left to the ladies. It was the custom to wash out and disinfect the room where the deceased had been ill as soon as possible. Some of the ladies scoured the walls and floor while others washed the dished and furniture with lye soap.

Some members of the family took afternoon naps to prepare for all night wake. There were prayers before and after supper that resembled a church supper.

As darkness approached, the wagon brought Cabel's body from the cave to the house among more prayers and hymns.

Henry Jr. had walked out to the yard and was leaning on the fence when his father, Henry Sr., saw a worried look on his face. He went over to talk with him. Henry Jr. was not only grieving the loss of a fine son but was worried about feeding his large family of thirteen with only three of the boys old enough to do farm work. Cabel was just old enough to do a man's work when he died. Also, from what he had heard, the wheat crops were failing all over the county.

Henry Sr. talked to his son and told him to remember all the hard times that they had had.

"Remember the winter of 1799 when the panthers and wolfs had killed all their livestock and the family survived? Remember 1816, when ask filled the sky and we didn't have a summer that year, couldn't grow a thing, and people survived on deer meat that winter? We all thought that the world was coming to an end. You were twenty-four years of age and had just married Polly that year before and your daughter Rebecca was born in June of 1816. There is not a family in Lillydale that has not lost at least one child. We'll worry about the farm and family next week, it's important that you get your grieving done now."

Just after midnight, Henry Sr. rose and talked with the mourners. He thanked them for coming and the whole family appreciated all of their help. He suggested that they all get some rest for he wanted to talk with his grandson for a while.

"We will be fine, after all, who ever heard of Judgment Day coming in the middle of the night?"

The preacher arrived by horseback the next morning before they had finished their breakfast. He wanted to talk with the family as soon as possible. He said a lot of kind words and told them that Cabel was now in God's hands and he would be taken care of. The preacher would hold services at the gravesite, as there were no churches in Lillydale.

They did have a beautiful hill top cemetery, not only overlooking Lillyday, but with a wide view of Peter's Mountain. A more "God-like" site could not be found.

At the service, Mary Jane tried to comprehend as the preacher spoke. He said, "dust thou art, and into dust shall thou return. The body returns to the earth from which it came."

The preacher prayed;

"Oh Lord, we bless thy holy name for all thy servants who depart this life in thy faith and fear, beseeching thee to grant them continued growth in thy love and service."

She was able to hold her tears until the singing.

"Now labor's task is over;

Now the battle days have passed;

Now upon the Fathers shore lands the voyager at last... "

Tears kept Mary Jane from hearing anything else that was said. She looked at her brothers and sisters and was so glad they were beside her.

That evening after the funeral Mary Jane wanted to be alone with her thoughts. She didn't know what the others were thinking, but she couldn't stop thinking of her mother.

CHAPTER TWO

Mary Jane's life had changed on Wednesday March 6, 1833, as her father had married Elizabeth Kessinger. The Kessinger family was of German origin also, but they had come to Monroe County about twenty years before the Arnotts came. They originally spelled their name as "Kisner" but Monroe County has a way of changing spellings. For some reason, Mary Jane had trouble thinking of her as mother.

Elizabeth was thirty-three years of age when she married Henry Jr. and she took on his nine children to raise as Henry's oldest daughter Rebecca had married Jefferson Mann in January of that year. The neighbors had said that step mothering is a hard business.

By the time, Henry Jr. had built two large rooms on to his house, one for boys and one for girls. He had grandmother's house, as he assigned an older child the responsibility of raising and caring for a younger child.

Henry and Elizabeth would have four children of their own:

Lucinda, born April 26, 1834
Caroline, born February 11, 1838
Jessie R., born September 5, 1839
John Wesley, born January 9, 1842

All babies were born at home without a doctor. Childbirth was marvel to Mary Jane. "Aunt Haddie" as she was called delivered most of the babies in Lillydale. She was known as the midwife of Lillydale. The neighbors all trusted her because they all knew she would send for the doctor if anything were wrong.

When the time drew near they would send for Aunt Haddie. Somehow she could predict the exact time of delivery. Some said it was witchcraft, others said women just knew these things.

If the time were near she would just move in with the family and stay through the entire event.

Mary Jane watched as she boiled the towels, made diapers from old rags, laid out soap, made homemade syrup with water, a tiny teaspoon, a knife to cut the umbilical cord and equipment to boil water.

As time approached, excitement built in the family; Mary Jane's job was to help in the kitchen so she held her post so that she could witness the entire event.

The mother was bathed well and given a dose of castor oil before delivery. Everything was laid out in proper order as Aunt Haddie made addler and black snakeroot tea.

After a labor that extended to what seemed forever, the child was born. The cord was cut and tied to the baby's belly and the baby was given a couple tiny spoons full of syrup and warm water. Then the mother was given a dose of paregoric and would remain in bed for nine days. Aunt Haddie would stay for the nine days but to only attend to the mother and child.

When the neighbor ladies came to visit, one of them said that they should have placed a knife under the bed to cut the pain of childbirth.

The normal payment to a midwife was to have a male member of the household go to the midwife's house to do work or to give payment in food, often a combination of the two. Aunt Haddie always said that she wasn't working for the family, but working for the Lord.

The workload increased at home as more children were born. Henry Jr. missed having Rebecca at home to help. He was having second thoughts about giving her permission to marry, as she was only seventeen at the time. But she was Henry's first daughter and she pretty much had him wrapped up. Or was it because Henry may have been thinking that a son-in-law would be more help around the farm? Jefferson Mann, however, was twenty-seven years of age and had a mind of his own, so they moved to a place down on Indian Creek.

Her brother Zachariah was close to Mary Jane in age and had a propensity for schooling. He would come home from school full of enthusiasm to show what he had learned. The older children showed him no attention so Mary Jane became proficient with American Primer and Webster's Spelling Book and doing figures from Pike's Arithmetic book. She caught on fast and was the benefactor of Zack's school learning.

Henry Jr.'s farm had been doing well even though he worried about the lack of help. Neighbors suggested that with Cabel gone he should buy himself a slave. He had heard that slaves would be sold in Union two weeks from Saturday, so he started to think about it. No one in the Arnott fam9ily had ever had a slave and all he knew about slaves is that they cost a lot of money and you had to feed them. He'd suppose that you could keep one like a member of the family and that he would work in the field and you didn't have to pay him.

Henry Jr. was sending a few cattle to market and selling most of his crops to the hotel at The Salt. The hotel would buy only the best of produce and farmers had such a hard time keeping up with demand to point that the resort bought its own farm on Turkey Creek to ensure it own supply.

The summer guests at The Salt had increased every year since the worldwide cholera epidemic of 1832 that hit the East Coast so bad. People said it started much earlier in Asia and worked its way through Africa and into Europe. Some said it started in Africa but if that were so then why didn't the Negro slaves have more immunity from it? One story was told that in Richmond, forty people died from cholera in one day and that three-fourths of them were slaves. Panic hit the coast and people left in droves, mostly to the mountains for the cool clean air and the mineral springs that had the reputation for curing what ails you. Even after the epidemic had passed on, increasing numbers of rich planters and land gently would come back to The Salt every summer. It also had the reputation of setting the best table among the Springs and it soon became the favorite of the people from the South Carolina coast.

Mary Jane's grandmother, Elizabeth, made the best Schmierkäse or cottage cheese around. She could also make spanfercel, kalbsbraten and apfelklose but, due to the lack of spices and ingredients available, she couldn't make them to her standards. But, cottage cheese she did make and plenty of it. The hotel liked it so well that on occasion they would send their own carriage twice a week to pick it up at Elizabeth's house.

When The Salt opened its own farm, Henry Jr. said,

"That's it! If I don't produce more on my farm they will buy less and less from us. I'm going to Union and buy a slave." If that's what he had to do then that's what he would do.

That Saturday morning he was up early and ready to go. At every opportunity he had he wanted Zack to learn the ways of the world so he told Zack and Mary Jane that they could go with him to Union to buy a slave. They were always ready to go at a drop of a hat. Mary Jane had a few coins saved up that she would exercise at Shanklin's shore while her father and Zack would get the news at the courthouse.

The slave auction would start in one hour and buyers were looking over the eight slaves to be sold. Some of the slaves were lame or injured, the older ones appeared to have arthritis and a "shifty-eyed" one had the scars of many lashes on his back. Why was this one whipped so much? Was he rebellious or had he tried to escape? As Henry Jr. stood among the potential buyers they began to grumble. One man said,

"These are culls that someone is trying to dump on small farmers."

The auction started and Henry Jr. made a low bid on a couple of them but soon backed off as few bids were made during the auctioneer's chatter. Something is wrong when so few people are bidding, he said to himself, so he backed off from buying and went to look for his children. Zack was excited by the prospect of owning a slave, but Mary Jane was shaken after seeing a human being sold at auction.

On the way home Zack was disappointed that they hadn't bought a slave as he had told his friends that they were going to. His father tried to explain to him that it wouldn't be wise to spend a lot of money on help that wasn't physically or mentally strong. He said to emphasize his point that a fool and his money will soon part. Zack thought for a moment and asked,

"Dad, how does a fool and his money get together in the first place?"

Henry had to think for a moment;

"A fool works hard for his money and then spends it on things that he doesn't really need, such as a sick slave. That's why I didn't buy one, besides; the children are growing and can do more work at home."

Little could Henry Jr. have foreseen what lay ahead. He knew that all the wheat crops were failing in 1836, which would mean that less labor was needed on the farm for wheat harvest, but with less bread they would have to make do with other items. Chestnuts would have to be gathered for roasting as they did when he was little boy when they first came to Lillydale. There is still plenty of game in the mountains. He talked about many things on their ride home from Union, but it all came back to one thing, his preoccupation with feeding his family!

He must have had it tough when he first came to Lillydale, the children thought. Henry Sr. was experienced in travel and surviving off the land, but his family was not. Their grandfather had told the stories many, many times in an organized manner, whereas their father told them stories as they occurred to him. He talked about the times when wild animals would kill their livestock and that they tried to raise sheep for wool to make their winter clothes but the wolves and mountain lions killed them off. Wool was so scarce that they had to rely upon trapping beavers to trade their furs for wool that were shipped in. Henry Jr.'s job was to find and cut fresh sassafras roots, as the beavers were fond of them. He even told about the lady down on Indian Creek who sat her baby down at the edge of her garden as she was working in it and a six-foot panther grabbed the child and carried it away. Only thing that was ever found was part of the baby's foot.

Henry Jr. grew up with the threat of Indians as the Indians were still in Monroe County when he was a boy. People carried guns with them to church and everywhere they went. Never did they travel alone unless they were on fast horse.

He also talked about the whole family walking seven miles one way past Union to the Rehobeth Church on Sundays. Preaching started whenever people would arrive and go on and on until the preacher got hungry, then they would have dinner on the grounds. Then preaching would start again and continue till it was time for the people to walk home before dark.

Since they didn't have a Methodist Church in Lillydale at the time and the Arnotts, Bakers and Weikles were devout Methodist, when they had a chance to hear a Methodist preacher they wanted to get all the preaching they could because it might be the last time for a while.

Most of Henry Jr.'s stories or sad, but he had two favorite stories that he would tell. When he was fourteen he was asked to join a cattle drive to market as they were shipping their cattle to Richmond. He talked about riding his horse and sleeping on the ground, as it was still warm that October. They drove the herd up past Union and out through Sweet Springs where they got to see the resort there. Then on down Dunlup Creek into Covington. It was exciting to drive cattle through towns and to keep then out of people's yards and gardens. They had a steer go up on a front porch once. They drove the cattle were loaded onto barges to be shipped to Scott's Station and then onto Richmond. Henry Jr. had wanted to go with the cattle and see Richmond, but that was the end of the drive and they returned home.

It was common in those days for people to stop in and check the health and needs of their neighbors. All day visits were ordinary and long stories of the past were told.

Other fond memories were the trips his family made down Indian Creek they turned left up Hans Creek to Ellison Ridge where Mr. James Ellison, a skilled weaver, had weaving equipment. People would go to his house to buy cloth to make their own clothes. On an earlier visit Henry Sr. had discovered that Mr. Ellison had also come from Sussex County, New Jersy, and even though Mr. Ellison was twenty six years older than Henry Sr. they became such good friends to the extent that their families would visit back and forth.

Henry Sr. was fascinated when Mr. Ellison told him the Methodist Church originated near Bohemia and Silesia, Germany and that's likely where the Arnotts came from, as they were Methodist before they came to America. Henry Sr. would have liked to have seen a map of Germany but there was none to be found in that part of Monroe County.

On the way home from Union, they stopped at the store at The Salt for no other reason than to get the local news. Mr. Seldon said that he had read in the Fincastle Newspaper that a New York Fellow by the name of Martin Van Buren had been elected President of the United States.

Henry Jr. asked; "How will that affect me?"

"Well the United States controls the banks and the banks control the economy! Our economy (the resort) is just across the creek." Mr. Seldon replied.

"If the resort buys good then times are good, if they don't then times are hard." Henry Jr. said.

Mr. Seldon then replied, "Maybe so, but I hear some complaints from the South Carolina guests that they are not happy with the U.S. government. They have nothing to complain about the way they throw money at the poker tables over there. Idle hands, I would say."

Two powerful U.S. Senators had visited the guests at Salt Sulphur Springs: Senator Henry Clay of Kentucky and Senator John Caldwell Calhoun of the backcountry of South Carolina.

They had teamed up before in 1817 when they convineced Congress to build The National Road from Cumberland, Maryland to Wheeling on the Ohio. "No small potatoes there."

John C. Calhoun had been proposing "Nullification," the non-acceptance of U.S. laws that were considered detrimental to the interest of his South Carolina. This was the tool that he used to counter the tariff interests of the northern states. Senator Calhoun stood at Salt Sulphur Springs like a noble Roman and moved the entire crowd with his Calhoun dialect, his intelligence and his sincerity that vibrated against the hills. Oh what a day in the history of The Salt! Mr. Erskins, the manager of the resort, was so moved that he named the new row of cottages that were being built on the hill "Nullification Row"!

In the 1830's Senator Henry Clay of Kentucky brought his "Whig Party" to Monroe County as a guest of Andrew Bernie. It had great appeal to the leading gentry in the country. His opposition to Martin Van Buren put him in good standing with the guests at the resort, even if the Protestant cleric wing of the party wanted to curtail the liquor trafficking. This didn't go well with some of the guests.

Mary Jane loved to watch the guests walk around at the resort. They were dressed as she had never seen before. She didn't know how to describe their fancy clothes. The gentlemen bowed to the ladies and they would curtsy in return. Servants brought from home followed them and even the servants were dressed finer than Mary Jane had ever seen. It all looked as if they were from another world and a fine world it must be. No work, plenty of money and servants to look after their every need.

Henry Jr. said, "We better get home, I'll have a lot of explain to do because I'm not bringing a slave home as everyone will be expecting."

By 1837 the number of guests for the summer decreased and folks said it was due to money crises at the banks in the cities and money was tight everywhere.

MR. SELDON SAID, "IT'S HARD TO TELL IF WE ARE IN A RECESSION AS MONEY IS ALWAYS TIGHT IN MONROE COUNTY."

CHAPTER THREE
President Van Buren

Early in 1838, Henry Sr. received his water mill that he had ordered from Baltimore. Now he could set it up on Laurel Creek and mill his own grain and saw his own lumber. Henry Jr. was also exited as it would save him all the time spent hauling his grain to Centreville to have it milled, plus there he had to give half of it to the miller to get it ground.

Henry Jr. never did buy a slave, so he was always looking for ways to save labor on the farm.

1838 was interrupted when word arrived that the President of the United States, Martin Van Buren, was coming to Salt Sulphur Springs for a visit. It seems that our Senator Bernie from Monroe County was a friend of the President and that he invited him to get away from the political heat of the recession and those awful summers in Washington, D.C. by taking a tour of the springs.

After a visit to Warm Springs, White Sulphur Spring and a night at Sweet Springs he was coming to Salt Sulphur Springs.

People were expecting an armed guard or an escort of cabinet officials but none were in attendance. He arrived in a plain carriage wagon escorted only by a driver followed by some locals who followed him from Union. His arrival was very common compared to the high style arrivals of the southern guests.

Senator Bernie and Mr. Erskine, the manager, greeted him at the resort. After two days at the hotel his reception was cooled by politics. It seemed that the northern states wanted tariffs on goods coming from Europe as they would protect their industries from being under priced, while the South wanted free trade with Europe as they had to import their manufactured goods. President Van Buren's wing of the Democratic Party was more interested in maintaining the protection for the northern manufactures.

So after a couple days of this he decided that he would rather talk with the local people this coming Saturday afternoon. He selected the very porch on the store where Mr. Seldon sits, so people could see him mixing with the common folks.

Well the word spread to Lillydale and everyone came early that Saturday morning.

President Van Buren, a widower, was a rather short plump man, banded with heavy, mutton chop side burns. His New York accent was certainly odd compared to the slow soft-spoken people around The Salt.

He was introduced to the crowd as having been a Senator from New York, Secretary of State and a Vice President under the most popular Andrew Jackson.

Henry Sr. was most proud the President was a fellow New Yorker.

In the introduction, Senator Oliver Bernie mentioned that "The President" was born in Old Kinderbrook, New York and his supporters formed the O.K. Club and began using the 'OK' to assure everyone that with President Van Buren everything would be 'OK' with America."

The kids picked that up right away and used "OK" to mean all right. It wasn't long after that that kids were dismissed from the supper table and sent home from school for saying, "OK" to their parents or schoolteacher.

Zack asked, "Is "OK" a bad word grandfather?"

"No". His grandfather replied, "but, I wouldn't try it out on your grandmother."

"Is it because she has been sick?"

"No, it's just not very respectful. If you want to get ahead in life, use yes air or yes ma'am to your elders and that will earn you more respect."

After the President's visit life went on as usual and they didn't really understand what the guests from South Carolina were complaining about as it was all too far away for them to be concerned. They would just leave Mr. Seldon to figure it out, as he never had much to do anyway.

Mr. Seldon said, "The Caololina guests were becoming more vocal in the affairs of Monroe County based upon the amount of money that they spent there."

Their latest interest was in the county militia. They wanted the county to increase the size of the two units, the 108th at Union and the 166th in the lower half of the county. They wanted the units to be a requirement of citizenship. Some said it was too much meddling but money talks. The rice and the fine "Sea Island" cotton money from the South Carolina coast supported The Salt.

By 1840 the recession was long gone and The Salt was filled to capacity. The Carolina guests claimed that the White Sulphur Spring Hotel was too boisterous and the mix of guests unsettling. They preferred the good manners of The Salt and the fact that The Salt Hotel served the best table of any of the springs. The Sweet Springs came close as they served the best mutton this side of England. Their guests were mostly from Richmond.

CHAPTER FOUR
Ralph Smith

Henry Sr.'s wife, Elizabeth had been in failing health for the past few months and she passed away on Wednesday, December 30, 1840 at the age of eighty. They say she just "wore out" but considering the hard life she lived, she should have worn out thirty years before. She had nine children in a log cabin and worked every day of her life.

"God will reward her," Henry Sr. said, as if his passing would be next.

Henry Sr. was able to get permission to have her funeral in the Stone Church at The Salt, and then bring her back to Lillydale for burial. The church was Episcopalian, but they had given the Presbyterians and the Methodists permission to use it for occasions in the fall and winter months. For the Arnotts, it was a privilege to be able to use such a fine church house.

Mary Jane was fifteen and proud of her family as she greeted all of her aunts and uncles at the wake. Her grandfather's mind seemed to be in another time.

She had worked hard preparing food for the crowd. William, her oldest brother, was twenty-three years of age, and had just gotten married. He took on the responsibility of notifying the neighbors and making the burial arrangements.

Mary Jane had also bought a lined notebook at Shanklin's store so her grandfather could see the list f those that signed in. In his state of mind he may not remember.

The guest list read:
Mr. & Mrs. Frederick Baker and son Andrew
Mr. & Mrs. Fraces Ellison and sons Joseph A.H. Ellison and J. Matthew Alexander Ellison
John, Joseph and Sally Baker
Mr. & Mrs. Jacob Pyles
Mr. & Mrs. Fisher
Mr. & Mrs. William A. Smith
Charles Jackson
Sara Fisher
Henry Pyles
Mr. & Mrs. William Weikle and son Samuel
Mr. Augustus McNeer
Mr. & Mrs. Canterbury
Mr. & Mrs. John Schrum, Salt Sulphur Springs
Note: Mr. Schrum, butcher at the hotel, brought a nice spring lamb already for carving and a jar of honey mint.
Mr. & Mrs. James Ellison, Ellison Ridge
Mr. B. Seldon
Ralph C. Smith
Mr. & Mrs. Fullen
Mr. & Mrs. Samuel Bare
Mr. & Mrs. Beckner

Family in attendance:
Aunt Martha and her husband Uncle Charles Neel Uncle William T. and Aunt Mary (were able to come in spite of her arthritis)
Aunt Nancy Rains
Aunt Sarah and Uncle Joseph Baker

Aunt Almedia and Uncle Levi Canterbury
(Too many first cousins to keep track of)

Mary Jane's immediate family of brothers and sisters:
  Rebecca and her husband Jefferson Mann
  William and his wife Adeline Dunbar
Elizabeth, age 22
Nancy, age 21
Joshua Franklin, age 20
Henry Watts, age 18
Zechariah Phillips, age 16
Addison Washington, age 12
Sara Truesdale, age 13
Her stepmother, Elizabeth
Lucina Arnott, age 6
Caroline, age 4
Baby Jessie R. age 1

Note: Aunts Elizabeth Wood and Deborah Neal, both in their upper fifties, had been sick this winter and were not fit for a long buggy ride in freezing weather.

The hotel manager sent a large holly wreath to the church.

Mary Jane just turned sixteen and was so good looking with her blue eyes and sandy blond hair. She was a little on the petite side, but tough as nails. She could cook a meal from scratch, harness and work a team of horses, load and fire a musket, sew her own clothes, put in a day's work in the fields, read a newspaper as well as help her step mother raise the children.

She was also shy due to the lack of social graces. Oh, how she missed her mother. She talked slow and didn't have much self esteem in public. She had grown to 5'4" and was beginning to fill out but not as much as the other girls her age. Her smile was nice, but the heavy housework while growing up gave her a slightly sad appearance.

Mary Jane had noticed that the boys were looking at her. She wondered why because her brothers paid no attention to her. One evening at a pie supper, she saw his boy, no attention to her. One evening at a pie supper, she saw this boy, no older than she was, continually looking back and smiling at her. He smiled and asked, "What are you smiling at?" He became embarrassed and slipped away without answering.

A couple weeks later at church, this boy sidled up to her and softly said, "I was smiling at you because I like you." Mary Jane's world changed again. He said his name was Ralph Smith and that he lived down on Back Creek toward Indian Creek. She went home that day as happy as she had been in a long time.

She and Ralph would look for each other at every event. Ralph shyly got up the courage to ask Mr. Henry Arnott Jr. if he could come calling on Mary Jane this Saturday evening. Henry Jr. reluctantly approved but he assigned a son to keep an eye on them every time they visited.

Soon they wanted to know everything about each other. Ralph had a good sense of humor with a little mischief. He loved to play tricks on her brothers but they never told her father because they knew that Mary Jane liked him so much. They liked him because he had the reputation of being a fine long shooter and he would give the boys tips on hunting. He showed them how to use Buffalo sticks to steady the musket for long shots. He would take two straight sticks about three feet long and in a sitting position he would hold the sticks in an "X" so he could rest the musket on them for a more steady shot. The sticks could be held from a kneeling or prone position.

Mary Jane asked, "How did you become such a good shot?"

He said, "That he was hunting with his dog when he was thirteen years old and we treed a bear. I shot the beer but only wounded him and at that instant the limb snapped and the beer fell on me knocking my breath out. When I recovered there was the bear sitting on me fighting with the dog. Something bit me on the ass and I came out from under the pile." On the way home, I said to myself, "I better become a better shot or I'll get hurt around wild animals. From that day on I went to work on becoming a better shot." His reputation spread as he could hit a target three to four hundred yards away.

Ralph lived at home with his parents Henry and Nancy Smith who had a large farm down on Back Creek. The Smiths came from the Valley of Virginia and had settled on Indian Creek about the same time that Henry Arnott Sr. had arrived. Over time they had acquired about eleven hundred acres. This was as much as Ralph and his brothers could work. They lived about three miles by road from Mary Jane or about a mile and a half through the fields. Ralph would just walk over to Mary Jane's house every Saturday evening or more often if Mr. Henry would allow. However, he began to wonder if he was always welcome, as Mr. Henry has turned a mean young bull loose in the field that Ralph crossed when he went to see Mary Jane. Ralph never knew if it was intentional or not, but it would take more than a bull to stop him from going to see her.

The field with the bull was about two hundred yards if Ralph would cross, and about six hundred yards if he went around the field. Ralph could easily judge distance as he was always practicing with his musket. About halfway across the field where Ralph would normally pass was a big stump and on the right side of the field was a small stream. The grass was always greener there, so there is where the bull would be most of the time. Ralph's choice was to either run across the field or walk all the way around it. After working all day on the farm, Ralph wasn't looking for any more walking so he worked out a plan. Ralph would sneak up to the field and quietly cross the fence to see where the bull was. If the bull was in his usual place and hadn't raised his head by now, Ralph would race to the stump, which was the decision point in the field. If the bull hadn't moved at that point he would dash on across the field to the other side. On the other hand, if the bull had started to run before he reached the stump, Ralph would turn around and go back to the starting place and then walk around the field. He always said that if that bull ever figured out dead reckoning that he would be in trouble.

The word of Ralph's Staurday evening run spread all the way to the guests at the hotel and they would ride out to watch the run. They would stand back from the field as to not "spook" the bull before Ralph arrived. Some of the guests said it reminded them of Pamplona—wherever that is!

In the winter when work was slow on the farm, Ralph found ways to make money. Whenever a farmer had a cow die, he would dig a hole and bury the carcass in return for the hide as pay. As soon as he had a load of hides he would take them by packhorse to a tannery at Narrows, down on New River and sell them for cash money. Then, of course, he would always bring a pretty gift for Mary Jane.

Cash money was always scarce around Lillydale but Ralph had told her that when he had enough money he was going to marry her. She was in agreement with that but they hadn't taken into account what her father would say.

By the time they were both eighteen, Ralph had grown about three inches and had developed the body of a mountain man, slim, muscular, with a healthy outdoor look. His reputation as a long shooter spread across the country and it wasn't long before the Kountz boys, the Weikle and Bare brothers were asking him to join them on their hunting parties.

They had been making money on wolf and panther bounties as well as selling hides and bear fat. They needed someone who could pick off a wolf across a hollow or high on a ridge.

It wasn't long before farmers were sending for them as they lost livestock, especially in the wintertime. Sometimes they would go on two or three day hunts. Bears were Ralph's favorite for they were a challenge. You had to be in good physical shape to hunt bear. There was the running, the fight and carrying the bear out of the brush. One of the Bare boys had a blue tick bitch that was the best bear dog you'd ever see. She would work with hand signals alone.

When food was scarce, an old male bear could commit depredation all over the countryside. The female bears would always go into dens but the male bears would feed through the winter. If bad weather happened, they would make a large bed in a laurel thicket and sleep it out. There would be nut-bearing limbs all over the place.

That dog could find cold trail and follow that bear ten miles until she treed him. Most of the time she would back off and let the men do the kill.

One time the bear made the dog so mad that she went in for the kill and got torn up so bad by the bear that she would only chase deer after that.

Some of the boys wouldn't shoot the bear in the head because they wanted to sell the head with the hide. They would try to shoot it in the heart but often missed because the heart is deeper and farther back in the chest than other animals, so they would have Ralph do the kill.

Since most weigh over two hundred pounds, they would only take the hide and fat and call the closet neighbor to come and get the meat. If the winter was cold enough they could have bear stew until spring.

Sometimes Ralph wouldn't get home until five o'clock in the morning.

At six o'clock Ralph's father would open his door and say, "Get up! You'll never make a George Washington laying there farting under the covers!"

CHAPTER FIVE

Salt Sulphur Springs

In 1844, both Ralph and Mary Jane were nineteen years of age. Ralph asked her to marry him. This was just a formality, as they both knew that sooner or later they would be married. So they planned for Ralph to ask Mr. Arnott for permission to marry his daughter.

He flatly said, "NO! Mary Jane is still needed at home as he older children are going out on their own."

"Besides", he said, "You do not have a home of your own nor do you have money to support her." Not only that, but he also announced that a well to do widower who owned a good farm had already approached him to ask for her hand in marriage."

Mary Jane and Ralph were shocked beyond belief, for she had not heard a word of this.

She had the constitution of her grandfather and with due respect she backed her father to the wall and announced for all to hear.

"First, there is no way on earth that I will marry some old angry widower and become a slave to someone else's children."

"Secondly, I am going to marry Ralph with or without your blessing."

Wall meets wall. Henry Jr. was floored by the thought that he too had been an angry widowed man and could have done the same thing to "Betsey," his second wife.

Dazed, he walked around the house to the barn to find a jug hidden there. Mary Jane grabbed a few things and asked Ralph to carry her to her grandfather's house.

It was a week ago, Sunday, when she and Ralph showed up at her father's house. They all met on the front porch. Mary Jane was ready for him, she told him to forget his pride and there would be no apologies this day and they would get down to business.

Mary Jane wanted a wedding with family approval, as it was such a large family. Her father was clam for he knew that to press his dominance at this point could lead to disaster. He sucked in his pride and approached the situation with a sensible demeanor becoming a man of his age.

His terms were that he would approve the marriage upon Ralph having land and a suitable house of his own and within a one-hour ride of his house. He knew that would delay the marriage long enough to Mary Jane to still help around the house and farm.

Ralph and Mary Jane walked down Laurel Creek to discuss his demands. Ralph said he would ask his father for some acreage as he had more than he could work now.

She asked, "What about your brothers and sisters? The farm is part theirs isn't it?" He said he would let his father work that out.

"How can you be sure?" she asked.

"Since Lewis and Clark", he replied, "there isn't a boy in Monroe County who hasn't talked about going west. Every time the Weikles and Kountz came by his house they talked about going to Missouri. In fact, half of the people in Raleigh County are from the lower end of Monroe County; some went on to Ohio. Not a father in the county wants his son to leave."

"And about the house?" she asked.

"I have a few hundred dollars now, and I hear they are paying good money for work on the turnpikes. I'll take my team of horses and work on the new turnpike they are building to Mountain Lake."

"I can help too," she said. "I'll work part time at the resort hotel in the summer and save money."

They discussed it for an hour with the maturity that only comes from the reality that hard work at an early age can bring.

They went back to the house and accepted his terms with the condition that Mary Jane be allowed to work at The Salt in the summers to accumulate some cash.

Henry Jr. consulted with his wife Betsy and Betsy liked the idea of having more time to herself around the house since the children were growing up.

Without argument or emotion he looked at them with respect and agreed to the conditions.

No date was set for the wedding, as there was far too much work to be done to meet the terms of the agreement. They now considered themselves a team with a mutual goal.

Ralph worked out an agreement with his father for thirty-seven acres; fifteen of which was cleared and the remainder had a good stand of timber. There was a house site on a knoll facing Back Creek.

He even had the idea of using the land as collateral for a loan to build a house. His father said that a three-bedroom house, as Ralph had wanted, with weatherboard siding would cost $1,500 at that time. Why it would be better than the house he was raised in!

His father also told him that if he were injured and could not work he could lose everything. Mary Jane would have to work as a "mid-wife" just to feed them. He also reminded Ralph that the only insurance that he had was the "Christian good-will" of his neighbors.

He went on to elaborate that there wasn't a bank close enough that would be able to lend the money to a dirt farmer in Monroe County and that men with money to lend in the county would crucify you if you were late with a payment.

"Just look what a lawyer did to the Halstead family down at the mouth of Indian Creek. He took their house and land because they couldn't make a $17.00 cash payment. The Halsteads had lived there for forty years and then had to up and move to Raleigh County to start over! No sir, never a borrower be!"

That evening Ralph went over to Mary Jane's house. He was sort of carrying the world on his shoulders.

Mary Jane asked him, "How much do you love me?" He thought for a moment and replied, "As much as meat loves salt." She was taken back by that answer and said, "That doesn't sound like a proper answer" and left Ralph standing on the porch.

The next day Ralph rode by her house and asked if he could cook dinner for her that evening. Now that was a surprise to her, but she said, "Oh, alright." He then asked Mrs. Arnott if he could use her kitchen to "cook supper for Mary Jane." She was so surprised that a man would want to cook that she was curious to see what might happen so she said that he could.

That evening Ralph arrived with food in a basket. The whole family wanted to see, but Betsy shooed everyone out of the kitchen. Ralph took out two one-inch thick prime steaks, and assortment of vegetables and some bread that was still warm as his mother had made it that day. Then salad and fresh homemade pudding.

Mary Jane said, "Then meat doesn't taste right." Ralph said, "You see meat loves salt." With that she got up and gave him a hug.

Mary Jane's next step was to get her grandfather to go with her to the resort to introduce her to someone who could give her a job. Henry Sr.'s first stop was to see his friend John Schrum, the butcher. He said there were always opening in the nangling but they wanted stout people to do the heavy washing and ironing.

Maybe in the dining room as the guests preferred attractive people in their presence. So he introduced her to Mrs. Gillard, mistress of the dining room. Mrs. Gillard was a tall, dignified lady who made you feel like standing up and saluting when she walked into the room. She agreed to start Mary Jane out cleaning the dining room after breakfast and lunch. She also said that Mary Jane would have to learn proper speech and manners before she could serve guests. She was to report to the kitchen at six o'clock am, Thursday through Monday, and would be finished by two or three o'clock. Take it or leave it.

Henry Sr. said, "Go ahead and take the job. I'll loan you a horse and clock to get started. Once you get your foot in the door, I'm sure you'll do fine."

At the hotel at the time was a "Miss Bee" Bonneau from South Carolina who was with the Entaw family as a tutor for their children. Miss Bee would work in the morning for the family but had the afternoons free. The manager, Mr. Erskine, was always looking for ways to improve the service for the guests, so he hired Miss Bee to teach his employees social graces for a couple hours each afternoon.

Mrs. Gillard said, "This is just what Mary Jane needs." At first Mary Jane was shy about all of this, but Miss Bee was not like most of the "uppity" guests. She seemed to understand the shyness of the local people. She was a character in her own right but easy to get to know. She was an experienced teacher having taught at the Beauford County Female Seminary until it was closed due to a yellow fever outbreak. Her job was to teach the half dozen in her class speech and manners that were acceptable to the guests. She understood their shyness in mixing with the guests and she would help them make their job easier. She told them that their speech was slow due to lack of social confidence. She also told them that their grammer was not improper, in fact it was legitimate because they inherited the Palatinate German dialect called "hock" Deutsche in which it was common to use prepositions at the end of a sentence. That is, "where is your house at?" is proper for those who have inherited this dialect. This dialect likely came from the middle Rhine Valley, a land ruled by Count Palatinate in 1356 AD. It later became attached to Bavaria in the 18th century.

Miss Bee brought a book of maps to the class, a book they had never seen before. She showed them drawings of the New World and of the Old World and pointed out Germany. The class still couldn't understand where it was until she explained to them that it would take six weeks to ride to Philadelphia, which Mary Jane had heard many times from her grandfather. Then they would have to board a sailing ship and sail for three months to reach Germany and another week down the Rhine River to where their people came from. To go there and back would take nine months.

Mary Jane said, "That's the time it takes to have a baby."

Miss Bee said, "That is not what we say in mixed company

Then Mary Jane understood what "Victorian" Meant, and why the hotel kept books by men and women authors on different shelves.

Miss Bee went on to explain that those prepositions at the end of sentences were not acceptable in the "King's English" and they should try to speak proper English, which she would try to teach.

"How does Miss Bee know all this," Mary Jane inquired for she was amazed.

Miss Bee explained that she had had the opportunity to study the classics when she was young. Also that her husband and daughter were drowned in a freshet on the wide creek near her home. She had lost the family, so she was in sympathy with the hardships of the local people. She also told Mary Jane that she reminded her of her daughter and wanted to help her.

She drilled them in how to stand, how to walk, how to greet guests and to only speak when spoken to, how to set a table and how to serve a drink. She taught them how to speak, which would take a lot of practice and she also taught them something far more important, and that was how to learn to think.

Mary Jane thought about this all the way home and she began to realize how it worked. You start with an object and work outward in all directions like spokes in a wheel. What is it, how did it get there, where did it come from, why was it there, and what can you do with it? These questions opened up a new way of looking at things for Mary Jane.

Miss Bee also taught them that if they thought of something strong enough, that the answer would come from their mind and that they would see things relating to that thought that they would not otherwise have noticed.

Mary Jane looked forward to these classes as much as she looked forward to her pay. She practiced the manners and speech so much that Ralph started to call her "Princess" which she liked but she also received cutting remarks from her neighbors and sisters-in-laws. They warned her, "Don't get above your raising." This hurt her, as she didn't mean to be uppity at all.

She replied, "One reason a puppy is such a loveable creature is that it wag its' tail instead of its tongue."

The men on the porch chuckled as those two badgered each other.

Soon as Miss Bee, Mary Jane and Mr. Burton, the storekeeper, stepped out on the porch, Mr. Seldon was ready for them.

He said, "I never could understand how it is that people living in the low lands can look down on people who live on a mountain."

Miss Bee replied, "It appeareth nothing to me but a foul pestilent congregation of vapors."

"What did she say?"

"Mr. Burton, that's that old Shakespeare talk that nobody can understand."

Mary Jane was making progress in the dining room and taking on more duties. However, she was also learning by her mistakes. In most cases the guests would let her know by showing their disapproval simply by raising their nose in a silent sneer. But when a guest complained to Mrs. Gaillard, Mary Jane really caught it. Like the time she served a guest Madeira wine chilled. Mary Jane didn't understand which wines were to be served chilled and which were not. Mrs. Gillard said, "I don't have time to train you. I'll have Bee give you a class on beverages."

Miss Bee brought two bottles, a bottle of wine and a bottle of port to teach them what the guests expect. "First of all", she said, "this is a bottle of Henriques and Henriques Madeira wine, a favorite since the Colonial days. It is produced on the Portuguese Island of Madeira off the west coast of Africa. Let's look at the map. It is shipped to the West Indies then up the coast to the States. It is one wine that is fortified or improved as it is rolled around by ship in the hot sun of the Atlantic Ocean. In fact, it is a favorite wine in England but they have it shipped to the West Indies, then back to England so it can improve by weeks of heat in the heavy ocean. This wine is not to be chilled! I emphasize this wine as it produces good money for the hotel. For example, the main meal is twenty five cents whereas a glass of Madeira is one dollar and fifty cents, so it is important that it be served correctly."

"The second favorite wine is Port, usually Quinta de Noval or Calem, from Porta, Spain. These are both red wines and again served at room temperature."

Mary Jane said that her grandmother would turn over in her grave if she knew she was serving drinks to a man.

She was always fascinated by the ways of the guests, but deep down she would never want to be one of them. To her they were people who never worked and lived off of the work of their salves. This just didn't seem right to the God that she knew. She did, however, like the gentle mannerisms of these folks who seemed to find more in life than the daily grind of living.

Business was booming at the hotel with over three hundred guests. The Erskine House was a sight to be seen with belles and beaus walking the portico porches that extended the full two hundred feet of the hotel. All seventy-two rooms were filled and slaves sleeping in the quarters under the building. Salt Sulphur Springs has thee fine springs: the Sweet Sulphur, The Salt Sulphur and the rare Iodine Spring. People were drinking from them, bathing in their waters or rubbing the waters on themselves for all sorts of healing powers.

It was an exciting time, sometimes a little too exciting, for Mary Jane noticed a gentleman guest by the name of La Chere hanging around her when she was working. She mentioned this to Miss Bee who replied, "Stay away from him, he is just looking for someone to pork while he is waiting for a rich girl to marry." How awful she thought, and then said, "If people think that about him and they see me talking to him, they may think that he is doing that to me!"

The very next day he approached her in the dining room and he asked if he could talk with her.

"No", she said, "I can't talk with you."

"Why not?"

"Because I am engaged to be married."

"So?"

"My friend is jealous and the best shot in the county."

"They all say that."

At that her temper ignited at his questioning her word. She shot back, "He can hit your left nut at three hundred yards!"

Mr. Le Chere could not believe a servant was talking him to that way. He would report her to the manager and have her fired.

He marched directly to Mr. Erskine's office and demanded to see him.

"Sorry, Mr. Erskine has gone to Union and will not be back until late."

Well he would just wait until he returned. He sat there that afternoon thinking about what Mary Jane had said — "ouch!" he thought, and all these mountain people have guns.

He remembered that last year one of the guests was taking his daily ride down Indian Creek and he would take a short cut on his way back, which happened to be through Mrs. Brown's potato patch. On his third trip, Mrs. Brown stepped out her front door and took a shot at him. He heard the ball whistle by his head and raced back to the hotel to demand that Mr. Erskine send for the sheriff to arrest Mrs. Brown for attempted murder. The sheriff rode out to see Mrs. Brown and after he saw her potato patch he came back and said that he could not arrest her for she only shot a warning shot in the air.

"She shot a warning shot in the air near my head!" he screamed.

Mr. La Chere mulled it over while he waited. If I get her fired her boyfriend may take a warning shot at me.

Two days later Miss Bee told Mary Jane that she could quit worrying as Mr. La Chere had left for White Sulphur Springs at first light. He didn't even wait for breakfast. It seems that he was pursuing Mr. Dehon's daughter when Mr. Dehon's slaves told him that Mr. La Chere was asking about how much land and how many slaves that Mr. Dehon owned.

Mary Jane realized that this place was a marriage market and that people married for money rather than love.

Miss Bee said; "Welcome to the real world, child. Come, let's go to the store and I'll buy you some candy."

As they approached the store there was Mr. Sheldon holding court on the porch.

When he saw Miss Bee he asked, "When are you going to invite me over to one of your fancy cotillions?"

"Never", she said, "you're too ugly."

"Well now, I can't help that can I?"

"Yes you can, you could have stayed at home."

She said, "If I were married to you I would give you poison."

"And if I were married to you I would take it."

There was a porch full of giggling and snorting as they entered the store.

Ralph's father paid him a wage for working on the farm that summer, but as soon as the corn crop was in the bin he went to work on the turnpikes that paid good money.

It was important to work on the roads before bad weather set in or they would cost more to repair in the spring. The roads were earthen, 18 to 22 feet wide with a crown in the middle for drainage. During the summer the crown would wear down and flatten. Water would stand on a flat road causing mud holes and washouts. If the roads weren't graded they would become impossible by spring.

The road from Sweet Springs to Union was well maintained, but the Indian Creek Draft also known as the Salt Sulphur Springs — Red Sulphur Springs Turnpike needed work and was under the supervision of Mr. John Vawter. This section of road ran from Union to Centerville where it split. One section going to Red Sulphur Springs and the other to Blue Sulphur Springs.

Ralph rigged up a grader pulled by oxen and a crew of three helpers to grade the road and to clean out the culverts.

Along Indian Creek he met people by the name of Estil, Mann, Millers, Kessingers and Cook. On past Centerville toward Red Sulphur Springs he met Meeks, Farleys, Bakers, Adairs, Johnsons, Ellisons, Harmons, Wilburns, Roles and Halsteads.

By Christmas time winter had set in and the turnpike work came to a halt. This would give Ralph and Mary Jane more time together. They counted their money and made plans.

Ralph said, "I can build our home and save money".

"By yourself?" she asked.

47

"My hunting buddies have volunteered to help."

"How will you build it?"

"That's what I want you to tell me."

"Tell you how to build a house?"

"No!" he said, 'which style of house do you want? The "German" plan or the "Virginia Hall" plan?'

"Like your grandfather's house?"

"What do you think?"

"Well, the German style with the fireplace in the center is much warmer in the winter as it heats the whole house but also is warmer in the summer while cooking. On the other hand the English Hall house is cooler in the summer as the fireplace is on the end of the house but in the winter it is warm on only one side of the house and cold on the other."

He suggested building the German style with a separate summer kitchen that could be used as a smokehouse in the winter.

"Great!" she said, "When will you start?"

"I've been hauling in some sandstone and with the central fireplace style we'll need to lay up the chimney first, then build around it. I can get Mr. Collins to build the chimney this winter as he is not busy at The Salt in the wintertime."

He said, "I know you want a weather board house but I'll have to build it with logs, then weather board the outside as we live in it. "

"Fine", she said, "a home is what you make of it."

"My father's house is on the Hall plan so I would like to see your grandfather's house again before I start."

"We'll cook dinner for him this Sunday and you can look at his house then."

Henry Sr. was proud that they were using the German style. "Let me show you. My original house was thirty feet wide and twenty feet deep with a useable attic. Then I added to the house when I put the weather board siding on."

"You see. There are two front doors, one to the "Stubes" or front room and one to the "Kuche" or kitchen as you call it. There is a hearth in both the Stube and the Kuche. The two rear kammers are the second and third bedrooms. The heat from the chimney keeps those two rooms warm."

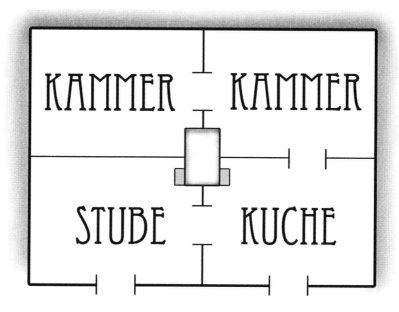

"If you get the chimney up and drag in the logs you should get it under roof before spring, then you can take your time with the finish work."

"Not too much time", Mary Jane added and Ralph chuckled.

He had his winter work cut out for him, except for a few hunting trips and time to dig some ginseng, as both would bring in cash money.

Mary Jane asked, "What can I do to help?"

"You can cook the bear fat as it is in great demand to water proof boots and for skin treatment."

Once they were focused on the goal of making money to build their house they were amazed at the many things they could sell for cash. They could sell feathers, bees' wax, Golden Seal, the "poor mans ginseng", and Ralph said the hotel was paying top dollar for lambs intestines to use as condoms.

Mary Jane said, "My word, don't let my family know what you are doing."

CHAPTER SIX
Building Their Home

Ralph's father had a slave by the name of "Trip" and there were three things that a slave should not do. Don't teach them to read and write, to learn to fire a gun and never let them have a drink of whiskey. Ralph and his brothers had taught Trip to do all these things and more. Henry Smith had seen the letters carved on the barn walls but figured his sons had done that.

Trip had made himself a member of the family years ago. Henry hadn't intended to own a slave, but one day in Union, Mr. Bernie approached him about buying Trip and at the time he needed more help on the farm as his boys were still young.

Henry said, "I'll tell you what I'm going to do. I'll rent this slave for a year." So they reached an agreement.

Trip worked out well as he was a good worker and caught on fast. Mr. Smith had treated him well and he liked living there. At the end of the first year, Mr. Smith took him back to Mr. Bernie and said,

"Here's your slave back."

Mr. Bernie said, "I don't really need him. Make me a reasonable offer and he's yours."

Mr. Smith studied on this for a moment. What's wrong with Trip that he doesn't want him back? Then it dawned on him.

Mr. Bernie has over a hundred slaves and Trip is too smart. He would give the other slaves ideas about working conditions and how they should be treated.

Mr. Smith said, "All I can afford is $150.00."

"Why that's half what he's worth! You worked him, you should know!"

"I'm not a rich man Mr. Bernie. That's all my small farm can support."

"Well, I'll take your money on one condition, that you get him out of town before quitting time. I don't want him coming around my slaves."

Mr. Smith and Trip chucked about it all the way home as that was the way both of them wanted it.

"By the way, where did you get that name Trip, anyhow?"

"They say that I was born on the same day as a big United States battle victory in a place called Tripoli in 1804. My owner took a fancy to that name and named me Tripoli and I've been called Trip ever since. I wonder if my name means that someday I'll takes a trip?"

By the time Trip was twenty-one, Mr. Smith said, "It is time that you had yourself a wife. Let's go pick out one for you."

"I done seen one that I like, she lives down on Hans Creek."

"Well, let's go get her for you!"

So that's how Trip came to jump the broom with Claire. Mr. Smith even built them a house on his place and they had two sons born in the 1830's.

Every time Ralph would go out hunting Trip would say, "I sure do like smoked turkey legs." One day Ralph said to Trip, "Why don't you go get one for yourself?"

"I can't catch no turkey with a fishing pole."

"That's right, you don't have a gun."

"None of us darkies have guns, don't you know that?"

"Well you are going to have my old 1831 Springfield musket and I'll teach you to shoot when I get back."

Ralph taught Trip how to load and fire and he could learn to hunt on his own.

"Just don't go showing it off to the neighbors."

"No sir, if they saw me with a gun they would shoot me for sure."

Speaking of guns, Zachariah P. Arnott, Mary Jane's brother, was after Ralph to join the 166th Virginia Militia.

Mary Jane said a flat "NO. Nothing interrupts Ralph until we are married."

The winter passed fast that year as they were working toward their goal. Mary Jane's sisters held a sewing bee for her to make quilts for her new home. Ralph said that he wanted to make the furniture out of chestnut so that it would be light enough for the children to push around the house.

Ralph and his crew dug the foundation and laid the rocks in place. Then they all helped Mr. Collins with the chimney. He preferred to work with creek rock of all sizes as this reduced cutting time. The boys were good, as they had a stone ready as soon as Mr. Collins had laid the last one. He used slaked lime mixed with clay for the mortar. This meant that they had to build camp fires on three sides of the chimney to prevent the mortar from freezing before it set up, which required them to keep the fires burning all night.

Ralph and his brothers had "snaked" in and trimmed the logs ready to build. He had bought new tools and even some store nails, which were very expensive. He had two broad axes; a new saw, mallet, auger, two new chisels as well as a new grindstone to keep the tools sharp. Trip had turned some replacement handles, as he knew young men like to show their strength.

Now it was a matter of waiting for a break in the weather and rounding up his hunting buddies to help him lay up the cabin.

His buddies called themselves "The Posse". A name they heard from out West and they were out to show that there was nothing they couldn't do.

Ralph was impressed. They were almost as good with axes as they were with guns. When they "lit" into the work it was all that Ralph could do to keep ahead of them. He was glad that he had laid out the logs in order. Locust for the sills and sleepers, poplar for the walls and pine for the rafters.

Trip set up his grindstone near where his young son was keeping a campfire going.

Ralph's plans were to get the floor joist laid, the walls and rafters in place and a thatch roof on until he could install a shake roof before the next winter.

That March day started cold, but sunny with no wind until later in the day. The young men worked fast to keep warm. Two chopping and carrying, two notching and fitting while Ralph would augur and pound in the pins.

By noon, with very little foolishness from the boys, (they were called boys until they were married); the house was taking shape. One of the Kountz boys let out with a wildcat yell that you could hear for a mile for he saw Mary Jane coming up the path on horseback with lunch. She too let out a cry at seeing the house take shape. When she got down from her horse she gave each of them a hug of appreciation for helping Ralph with the house.

She had brought a basket full of soda biscuits, pork shoulder sliced and fried and a pot of pole beans that she re-heated over the campfire. The crew devoured the vittles and pulled out their pipes to smoke. When Mary Jane left, the boys pulled out a jug and passed it around, then left the jug in reach of the grindstone in case Trip needed to warm up a bit.

By the middle of the afternoon, thin gray clouds were starting to block the sun. Trip said they were too high to have any snow. Ralph had hoped to have the walls half up and all the doors by now, but the locust lumber in the floor joist had slowed them down. As the sun had gone down Ralph said,

"Let's take a look of admiration as to what we have done today."

It was dark by the time they had gotten to Ralph's parents house where Mrs. Nancy Smith had fixed them a big meal of chicken and dumplings. Ralph's father had made them all a place to sleep.

After supper there was the usual story telling and some lying mixed in. They did agree that it would take another day and a half to get it under roof. Ralph began to wonder how he was ever going to repay them, as they wouldn't accept cash from him.

The poplar logs went up fast as the notching was easy and as the rafters went up Ralph realized that he was going to be short of thatch. He had hoped to have about a foot of thatch on his nine by twelve sloped roof, but with what he had he had to settle for six inches, which might leak.

The last day when Mary Jane brought their noon time dinner, she stayed around so that she and Ralph could thank them all as they headed home. When they were out of sight, Mary Jane took Ralph inside the cabin and rewarded him with a kiss that touched his soul.

A couple of nights later, at the supper table, Mary Jane's father said to her, "I thought you wanted a weather board house and you end up with a thatched covered log cabin." Mary Jane, as usual, was ready for him, she said, "It's all about love, Daddy."

By mid April 1846, work was well under way at the resort. The grounds were being manicured and flowers being planted. Everything had to be perfect, as the guests would be arriving by the first of June.

Mary Jane not only looked forward to making the extra money as their new house needed so much. She was also looking forward to seeing Miss Bee again. Surely she would be there this summer but you never knew for sure.

She thought that she better go to the dining room early to see if she still had a job; if not, she better apply for another one. As she walked to the store she heard some young boys playing in the yard between the store and the church.

They were singing;

"Hurray, hurray, it's the first day of May!
Outdoor screwing season starts today!"

As if they knew what they were talking about.

Mary Jane said, "God is watching you from that church steeple." With that the boys ran up the mountain road.

Mr. Seldon said to her, "Are you ready for the circus from the south?"

She replied, "I'll bet you're waiting for Miss Bee."

"No, it's been a peaceful winter."

"How far is it from here to South Carolina?"

"It's six hundred and seventy miles from Charleston to The Salt by the way of Fayetteville, Richmond and Staunton."

"See, I told you. You are waiting for Miss Bee."

At the dining room Mrs. Gaillard told her, "Yes, you do have a job, only because I don't have time to train another person."

Mary Jane thought to herself, "Next year you will have to train someone else because I'll be married."

The local men would gather on the store porch, especially on Saturday, the first of June. One fellow said that two carriages arrived late yesterday and we missed them. This was great entertainment, men just waiting to pass judgment on the arriving guest. Two old men sat there patiently, one said to the other, "Can you see that ant going up that tree across the creek?"

"No, I can't see him, but I can hear him."

Just then they heard the hoof beats of horses coming over the knoll. It was Mr. Walker driving one of the stages from White Sulphur Springs. The four galloping horses made a quick left turn over the bridge into the resort grounds.

Mary Jane said that couldn't be Miss Bee as the family she would be with would have a spring carriage followed by a light Dearborn wagon with luggage and slaves in it.

Guests meant work so she checked into the dining room to assume her assignment.

In less than a week Miss Bee arrived and they were both glad to see each other. She was with the same family. The children had grown and they had a new slave with them. A very tall, slim lady who was very black, unlike anyone that Mary Jane had seen before.

The resort had grown so popular that guests who arrived without reservations were often turned away and sent to other springs. Some to lesser springs such as Grey Sulphur Springs in Giles County and Yellow Sulphur Springs near Blacksburg. Guests arriving late in the day often had to seek shelter with local farmers. Mr. Erskine had assumed considerable power as he was in a position to say who stayed and who couldn't. He always favored the guests from the coast of South Carolina as they were the big spenders and were more loyal to Salt Sulphur Springs.

As the popularity of The Salt grew, it became more fancy. Some ladies would take up to two hours to dress for dinner even with the help of their slaves. It became a serious marriage market with unbelievable social knifing, and the men joked, "that for every back there is a knife."

Miss Bee came by the dining room and Mary Jane asked about her trip to the retreat. "Did you come by Richmond?"

"No, we came from a different part of South Carolina, whereas many of the guests stop in Charleston to socialize and shop on their way to the Springs. We came directly from Beaufort County. We came by way of Columbus to York, South Carolina, Lincolnton, North Carolina, and Danville to Rocky Mount into Sweet Springs. When we return, we will go by the way of Giles County Court House, Salem, Henry County Court House to Rock Hill,

South Carolina, Columbus and home to Beaufort County and the low country."

"Our people are mostly Protestant Huguenots whose ancestors escaped persecution in France. My ancestors came to America and settled at Port Royal in the early 1700's. That area is made up of rich farmland, islands, rivers and swamps that get very hot in the summer time. Our families have large plantations with many slaves. In fact eighty percent of our population is slaves. We grow rice, indigo, sweet potato and the finest Sea Island cotton in the world!" she said proudly. "When you hear guests by the name of Screnen, Le Clerce, Pringle, DuPont, Manigault, Guerard or Dani-ell they are likely to be from Beaufort County and are rich land owners."

"Unfortunately, the summers are very hot and it is difficult to survive because of the mosquitoes, malaria and yellow fever. The wealthy plantation owners usually leave in April after the planting is done and do not return until the first frost in November. This gets us past the heat and hurricane season. Christmas season is wonderful there."

"But who takes care of your farms?"

"Our slaves do, and sometimes we have to leave slaves in charge of slaves."

"Don't they get sick?"

"Yes, some of them do and some of them die, but we have so many that life goes on."

"There we travel as much by boat as by carriage. We travel the rivers and swamps to visit our neighbors and even to Charleston. It can be the best life or the worst."

"My husband and daughter, who would now be your age, died in a freshnet."

"What is a freshnet?" Mary Jane asked.

"It's when a storm causes a sudden rise in shallow water causing boats to capsize."

"I'm so sorry!" Mary Jane said.

"Let's go over to the store and see if they have anything new."

At the store Mr. Seldon was so excited to see Miss Bee that he made an awkward step toward her.

"Pray eleminetc word stand far from me," she said. "I will give thee bloody teeth."

Mr. Seldon asked, "Does Shakespeare live in South Carolina?"

"More of your conversation will infest my brain," as she winked at Mary Jane.

It was good to have Miss Bee back.

The summer of 1846 did drag on for Mary Jane and Ralph, as they had a lot on their minds. They were both twenty-one and had met her father's conditions for getting married but her father wasn't sure so he let it drag on.

Working at The Salt had been very enlightening for her. The new slave lady was called Maum Mary and she spoke with a West African dialect that was very difficult to understand. She called women "Ooman" and men "Mahn". She was very talented and the family loved her "gumbo" and "okra" African dishes. Actually, the family brought her to the resort to show her off. Mary Jane enjoyed all this but the urge of motherhood was growing.

Instead of Ralph going to see Mary Jane, they would meet at the house and she would help him put on the shingle roof. She would carry the shingles up the ladder for Ralph to nail on. The split cedar shingles had to be nailed on when the points of the crescent moon were pointing down. To install them when the moon points are up would cause them to curl and split. So they had to work fast. Once the roof was on they could lay the flooring. By frost, Ralph and his crew were back to work on the turnpikes. He needed the cash for his new house.

Henry Sr. had several sick spells during the winter and Mary Jane stayed with him several times. He was eighty-five years of age, remarkable to live that long in an age where most men had an average life span of forty years.

That Christmas Eve, Ralph gave Mary Jane a gold wedding ring.

"My, what an extravagance!" the family said.

For wedding rings were out of reach for most families in Lillydale. But Ralph also wanted to send a message to Mary Jane's father.

By late March, they were able to plow the garden and get their potatoes in. Neighbors frequented by to see how they were doing, always ready with advice to the point of aggravation.

One reminded them that, "There's a time for everything, a time to be born, a time to die, a time to plant and a time to harvest. That's God's book. The signs work because they are in God's plan when he made the earth.

" Mary Jane asked her father if they should be planting in the signs?

And he said, "I think you should but if you take too long to plant you're bound to run into some bad signs."

A neighbor came by one day and asked, "Ralph, what sign did you plant your beans in?"

Ralph replied, "I planted them in the ground."

"Now Ralph, be nice. We'll have to live with these neighbors a long time." Mary Jane said.

The neighbor then said, "These are the signs of the Bible. I guess each generation has to learn by doing to become believers."

Dr. Butt from Centerville had been making frequent trips to see Mr. Arnott in his tall-wheeled buggy that could ford the creeks and wash outs in the road. He told the family that with his age there wasn't much that he could do except leave some medicine and instruct the family on how to keep him comfortable. The neighbors were looking in more frequently and bringing him food.

One Sunday, Henry Sr. called for Mary Jane and Ralph. He told them, "I want you to go ahead and get married. You have waited long enough."

"Thank you for your blessing." They said, "We love you very much."

The grandchildren had been taking turns caring for him. Mary Jane would stay with him on Sundays to let her older brothers and sisters have more time with their families.

On Tuesday, May 26, 1847, Henry Arnott Senior departed this world. He was surely loved, not only by his large family but also by caring friends and neighbors. Many people would attend his wake and funeral as people always felt better when doing something.

They would set up for the wake and sing hymns. They brought food and sometimes there were so many people in the house that the boys could stand in the corner and sleep.

The family paid six dollars to have a coffin made. When they loaded it on the wagon to take to the church at Salt Sulphur for the funeral.

The preacher made the remark that, "Mr. Henry had traveled this road so many times in the past fifty years that he knew it like the Lord's prayer."

They rang the bell and the preacher conducted the service in the church. Following the service they lifted the lid from the coffin for viewing. The neighbors filed by, followed by the grandchildren and children. This was a very hard part for Mary Jane for funerals were very upsetting to her.

At the end of the long procession back to the cemetery at Lillydale, a lady said to her husband,

"You know, we need a church in Lillydale."

"No we don't." he said, "If we have a church then they will want a Post Office and with a Post Office it will make it too easy for people to find me."

Mary Jane and Ralph discussed their wedding plans.

Ralph asked, "Are we suppose to wait three months after the funeral before getting married?"

"Not in this case, for it's what he wanted. We'll wait six or seven weeks", said Mary Jane.

Miss Bee was able to arrange for the wedding to be held in the church at The Salt. She could only arrange it to be on a Thursday as the guests had activities there on Saturday and Sunday. Mary Jane had the option of having it on a Thursday or having it at home on her front porch on Saturday. She had always admired that church so they set the wedding date for Thursday, July 17, 1847.

Her sisters and friends helped with the details and they selected dogwood for the theme. Mr. Erskine loaned them a fine open carriage to carry them to and from the church. Since the church had an organ they could have singing.

The church was filled that fine July day, just perfect weather. The flower girls, Amanda Smith, Carolina Arnott and Rebecca Baker, sprinkled dogwood blossoms as her father walked her up the aisle.

About all she remembered was when Reverend William Crook asked her;

"Do you take Ralph Estil Smith to be your lawful wedded husband?"

It was like an end to a long journey. She did notice as she came out of the church that Miss Bee and Mr. Seldon were sitting beside each other on the same bench.

What a beautiful ride it was back to their new home in Lillydale. The young folks had decorated their home with ribbons and wreaths. There were plenty of refreshments and all their neighbors came and stayed until they had an open-air serenade for them, then everyone went home.

Finally they were alone. Ralph was so shy that Mary Jane had to tell him to get naked with her. Then he became a man.

It wasn't very long before Zack came by recruiting for the 166th Militia. Zack had been elected 2nd Lieutenant for his recruiting and politics. Ralph agreed to join, as it was a civic-minded thing to do. They would meet once a month for drill and training. He enjoyed the fellowship and news but he didn't care much for his brother-in-law telling him what to do.

In 1848, two things happened. Mary Jane and Ralph had their first son. There wasn't any doubt as to what they would name him, Henry Alexander of course!

Secondly, that summer was hit by a terrible drought. People would hang the body of a snake, belly up on a tree limb, to bring rain. The crops were half their normal size. Mr. Erskine had to send as far way as Zenith for vegetables to meet the demands of the guests.

It got so bad that snakes were coming out of the mountains looking for water. Several people and livestock were bitten. The dogs were good at warning; still Mary Jane had to be very careful with young Henry outside.

Their son Henry was almost three when their second son James Preston was born in 1851. They intentionally were spacing between the births of their babies, for a child born every year was hard on the mother, as it had been on Mary Jane's mother.

Zack would come by with a newspaper that was now being published in Union. He also told them about a Temperance Movement that was sweeping the country. He urged them to go to The Salt to hear Governor John Floyd who was due to speak there.

CHAPTER SEVEN
The Boys

Mary Jane and Ralph's third son Wilson G. was born in 1853 and they had their hands full on the farm. In addition to foods of all sorts, it was necessary to find and have a supply of home remedies on hand. Ralph was good at finding roots and herbs. He always had a good supply of dried leaves for tea and hore-hound for colds and sore throats. They would take turns with their neighbors raising sugar cane and it became a community event when it became time to make sorghum molasses. The farm was good to them and they had a happy life.

More and more it seemed that politics were the main subject of the day at The Salt. Eventually everything that was said at the resort ended up on the store porch. Most people didn't take too much interest in it, what they seemed to hear was that the northern states wanted to tell the southern states what to do and on top of that they wanted the south to free their slaves.

"What difference does it make to us?" one fellow said, "We don't have any slaves and we certainly don't have any tariffs."

"Well the south is on shaky grounds for you know the Lord's not going to put up with these people who are gambling ten thousand dollars a day at the hotel while slaves are making their living."

Mr. Seldon allowed, "Any way you figure it, politics is war, and if you mix politics with business, business will suffer."

The conversation heated up.

"Well, I consider myself a citizen of Virginia above being a citizen of the United States. I know I'm a citizen of Virginia first."

Another fellow said, "I'm not so sure about that. Didn't the big wigs in eastern Virginia vote in favor of the canals over railroads? The canal stops at the James River, which limits access to the market for Monroe and Greenbrier counties."

"They did it because they don't want competition. They could have had the railroad over here by now."

"We are supporting a state that's working against us."

"Well for now," a gentleman spoke up, "I know which side my bread is buttered on, so I'm sticking with Virginia."

"Little do they know what's ahead" Mr. Seldon muttered to himself.

For now, the guests were happy with their balneotherapy and their quadrilles.

The Salt Sulphur Springs Company didn't wait for Virginia to build roads. It had built its own private toll road, Salt Sulphur-Mountain Lake Turnpike, which was forty-eight miles long and it extended to the Lynbrook Hotel at the base of Salt Pond Mountain.

On Wednesday January 20, 1858, weighing seven and a quarter pounds, a son Robert Estil was born to Ralph and Mary Jane. Mother and child were doing well with plenty of family to help out. Older brothers Henry age twelve, James Preston age eight and Wilson G. age five were all disappointed, as they wanted a girl.

Ralph was taking on more responsibility in managing and working his own farm as well as managing his father's farm. Fortunately, his boys were big enough to help with the chores.

Henry and James were walking to school in Centerville four months out of the year. It was two and a half miles one way but they enjoyed walking with the other children. Mr. Henderson Ellis, the teacher, was a man of discipline, and if the parents heard about any trouble at school they would also be punished at home. Ralph would cut a switch and warm their pants but Mary Jane was more kind. She had a wooden bucket that she would fill with rocks and make the boys carry it around for an hour or two.

Trip and his wife Clair had three children, two boys and a girl, all a few years older than the Smith boys. With the help of the Smiths, Trip was training them for the world ahead. Trip had taught them all how to live off the land and his daughter was helping Mary Jane and learning all she could. Trip had told them many times that he had a bad feeling in his bones, that there would be hard days ahead.

Ralph's father Henry Smith had given Trip his freedom three years ago and now was paying him a wage plus the use of the house, which he had always lived in, and a garden.

Trip was happy on the Smith farm but he knew that his children would be moving on one day.

Life on the farm was good. Ralph had put the weatherboard siding that Mary Jane had always wanted on the house and painted it white. They were making money-selling produce to the hotel and Ralph converted his paper money to gold and silver. He just wasn't fond of paper money. The farm had good fruit trees and a large garden. They also raised some cattle which required hay and corn crops.

In addition to selling to the hotel, they bartered for most things that they needed. The store at The Salt would trade for ginseng, wool and furs. Ginseng was a very profitable business. As evidence, Mr. Bernie near Union made a fortune buying for a Philadelphia company that shipped tons of it to China.

Ralph was no longer working on the turnpikes, as the fall became a very busy time of the year on the farm, with making apple butter, molasses and cutting timber. He did take time to teach the boys to hunt and how to find ginseng. He showed them the locations of his regular areas that he harvested every fall when the colors of the berries were just right. He showed them where ginseng grows best in a shaded high moist area on the north side of large trees.

Even though Ralph kept bees, it was always a delight to find wild honey as the old timers preferred it to home raised honey.

There was so much to learn on the farm that the boys were kept busy all the time and it helped them to mature fast.

They had to learn how to take care of the horses, how to butcher hogs, and skin animals to take their hides to the tannery in Centerville or to the Narrows on New River.

Trip had a wooden shoe cast that he made himself and from it he could make a pretty good work shoe. The only problem was that both shoes were just alike and could be worn on either foot. Mary Jane insisted that their dress shoes be made by Mr. Bare at The Salt from good cowhide.

Since Mary Jane's uncle was a trustee at the Methodist church in Centerville, Henry Arnott insisted that the family go to church there. The world for the folks in Lillydale seemed to be split between Centerville and The Salt. For the most part Ralph preferred to trade at Centerville because he knew more people there, but he would go to The Salt to pick up his mail and a newspaper.

Lately he didn't like what he was hearing there as it was too much politics.

One thing he did like about The Salt was its influence on the old German cooking that Mary Jane was raised on. Some of the things that the folks from South Carolina introduced to local cooking were;

Fricassee Chicken	*Salted Fish*
Chili Sauce	*Scalloped Tomatoes*
Tomato Catsup	*Okra*
Rice Pudding	*Wine Sauce*
Macaroni	*Watermelon*
Omelets	*Peanuts*

Plus a good helping of table manners.

CHAPTER EIGHT

The Thunder of War

By December 1859 the county leaders in Union worked the people in the county into a fever of excitement from speeches. Especially when they heard of John Brown's raid on the Federal Arsenal in Harpers Ferry. He had invited the slaves to revolt. This struck fear in the hearts of many and the politicians used this to their advantage to promote the southern cause.

Trip was very worried, but Ralph reminded him that he was no longer a slave and that he had a safe place to live for the rest of his life. Trip said that he thought of sending his children to Ohio.

"They may have more opportunities there."

Ralph's mind was at home, for on Sunday, December 20, 1859, Mary Jane presented him with their fifth son, Erastus P. Smith. This time Mary Jane was disappointed as she was hoping for a little girl.

Anyway, it was a joyous Christmas for the whole family except that Henry and James P. had made fireworks by hollowing out corncobs and filling them with gunpowder and lighting them in the front yard which woke the baby.

In January, Dr. Nowland ordered the school in Centerville to be closed due to a typhoid outbreak. To add to her chores at home, Mary Jane would take two hours out of her busy day to teach the boys at home. She asked her brother Zack to come by for three hours each week to test the boys in arithmetic and reading the newspaper. Then he taught them beyond reading and writing. He taught them government and the world beyond Monroe County.

The boys would talk about what they wanted to be when they were grown. Henry said he wanted to be a farmer like his father and in many ways he was like his father — quiet, mature for his age and could do most anything on the farm. James Preston, on the other hand, always talked about going west to become a cowboy. He was more outgoing, more rambunctious with a quick temper and with a tendency to get into more trouble. Like the time when he was eleven years old. He found a den of copperhead snakes under an old rotted tree stump. He took about a half-cup full of his father's black gunpowder and poured it in a crack in the stump. As soon as he lit it, it blew him and the stump over the bank. Mary Jane had to send for Dr. Nowlan in Centerville to come and treat him. He was still blind for two days after that.

Another time when they had a sick calf, their father sent James and Wilson to sit up with the calf over night to make sure the calf didn't get down and die. He gave the boys some coffee and a bottle of brandy for the calf. The boys gave the coffee to the calf and drank the brandy themselves. The next morning when their father went out to the barn he found the calf well and the boys sick.

Wilson G. was a good boy; he wanted to be a teacher or maybe a preacher. He was a good worker with plenty of ambition.

Their Uncle Zack was always going to Union where politics was talked day and night. "What should we do about the national crisis? Many feel that we should stay out of it, others say that the cotton money feeds us through Sweet Springs, Red Sulphur Springs and the Salt Sulphur Springs and that Virginia is our mother and as a citizen we must protect Virginia. Whichever way Virginia goes, I will go."

Many were split over the slavery issue. The wealthy in the county favored slavery since so much of their wealth depended on slaves, whereas some of the small farmers didn't think it was worth dying over.

After a political debate in Union, two gentlemen from Lillydale were riding home.

One said to the other, "You sure missed a good opportunity to keep your mouth shut."

At that they both rolled off their horses and had a good fistfight right there in the road. When it appeared to be pretty much a draw, they got back onto their horses and rode home without saying nary a word. They both came to the realization that the same thing could happen between the states.

Zack was very busy with the Militia recruiting and organizing drills. He was promoted to Lieutenant Colonel and Ralph to 3rd Sergeant in Co. E. 166th Militia. Drills were normally once a month, now they were every Saturday. The fine for missing a drill was twenty-five cents. Some said that Centerville got its name, as it was a central location for the 166th Militia to meet.

As this year's crop of guests rolled into the hotel there was crazy excitement. Some guests even brought uniforms and held drills on the resort grounds.

There was talk of the Union freeing slaves who would then turn on their owners. This caused great concern and anxiety to the local people. Some declared that they had seen visions in the sky and in nature. One person said he saw a leaf with "W" on it, which meant war.

Miss Bee came to see Mary Jane every couple weeks and brought gifts for the babies. She was very concerned that if war came this could be her last summer at The Salt.

CHAPTER NINE

War Begins

Every other day it seemed that the men folk found some reason to go to The Salt but the real reason, of course, was to hear the news, which mostly came from the Fincastle newspaper.

The real news was that General G. T. Beauregard of South Carolina had ordered the bombardment of the U.S. Fort Sumpter in Charleston Harbor. He said, "Those fellows from South Carolina have really done it now. There will be hell to pay."

Mr. Erskine said, "You better be thinking of what it will do to the hotel business. How are they going to fight and still come up here for the summer?"

Mr. Seldon said, "Why I remember that Pierre Gustane Toutant Beauregard making a speech from this very porch last summer. I could have told you then that he was a trouble maker."

As soon as word reached Washington D.C., President Lincoln declared war on South Carolina.

"He might as well have declared war on Salt Sulphur Springs. Without the South Carolina guests, The Salt is dead," Declared Mr. Erskine.

The headline news from Fincastle was "Virginia joins the Confederate States." The politicians in Union went crazy. They raised a flag with the St. Andrews cross, which was the first Confederate Flag that most people had ever seen.

Ralph went home to tell Mary Jane the news and they sat up half the night discussing what might happen. They didn't have to wait very long, for Zach came by at breakfast time and was all excited as he was calling out the 166th Militia to assemble in Union. Ralph took him in, sat him down and in no uncertain words told him that he would attend the meeting and fight in the defense of his home county, but he was not going to leave the county to fight. "This is not our war, we have nothing to gain and everything to lose."

"The county needs you", Zach said.

"My wife and children need me. My elderly father and mother need me. Your father Henry is elderly and he needs me. You see, my family needs me more than the county needs me."

The summer of 1861 saw a surprisingly large crowd at the resort, mostly made up of women and children as the men had gone to war. There even was a large number of ladies from Richmond there as they had left to get out of harm's way. Some talked about spending the winter there, but never did.

The farmers who feared that they would lose business from the hotel found that they could sell anything and everything to the Confederate Government. Prices were highly inflated and some items such as coffee, sugar and salt became scarce. Ralph rode a horse and led another one to the salt works on the Kanawha River and brought back two hundred pounds. This seems like a lot of salt but when you're curing meat it doesn't go far.

There was a lot of excitement at The Salt when Mary Jane and her boys went to pick up the mail. Word had just arrived that the Confederate Army had won a major victory in a place called Manassas. Some said it was so close to Washington that they should have gone ahead and captured Lincoln. This was so encouraging to the guests that they planned a big celebration and even invited the local people.

"First time that every happened!" said one fellow.

"They should!"said another. "For five Monroe County men were killed in that battle."

Mr. Seldon and Mr. Well, the storekeeper, went to the celebration dance. The next day.

Mr. Wall said "Mr. Seldon wanted to dance with Miss Bee in the worst way and he did."

The Post Master showed Mary Jane a notice to the public from the Confederate Government that all citizens of the Commonwealth were to turn in all silver and gold money in exchange for Confederate currency, meaning paper money. "Ralph will raise hell when he hears this." She thought.

"They are going to have to shoot me first." Ralph said. "If the south looses, the paper money will be worthless." He thought on it for a time and came up with a simple plan. "I will turn in a small amount for Confederate currency, enough for immediate needs and bury the rest on the hill where only Mary Jane will know where it is. It's none of the government's business how much money I have."

"But it's war!" she said.

"Well, I didn't start it. That money is for you and the boys."

As it turns out they would need that money for Mary Jane had their sixth son, Anderson P. Smith, in 1861. The Lord works in mysterious ways, for as one is born another is taken away. Mary Jane's brother John Wesley Arnott, age 19, died on Saturday October 19, 1861.

The next month, Henry Arnott's wife and Mary Jane's stepmother died on Friday, November 29th. And in the following month another brother, Addison Washington Arnott died on Sunday, December 22nd of that same year. Oh, what a sad Christmas for the Arnott family. It was very hard on their father, Henry Sr., age seventy. He tried not to show it but neighbors said that he had aged ten years in the past three months.

CHAPTER TEN
The Neighbors

In January 1862, Mary Jane received a letter from Miss Bee telling her of the disaster that had happened in Beaufort County, South Carolina. On Thursday, November 7th, seventy-five Union vessels, including seventeen war ships and two thousand infantry, had arrived at Port Royal Sound, invaded Beaufort and also captured Fort Walker on Hilton Head Island. Many planters had fled to Charleston and the slaves were now living in their master's homes. Her family had taken heavy financial loses as well as most of their neighbors. It was very unlikely that she would return to The Salt again. "My best regards to everyone there and God bless you and your children." There was no return address.

Mary Jane showed the letter to Mr. Erskine, he said, "Half of my guests are from Beaufort County and I've gotten to know them quite well over the years." He thought a moment and said, "The excitement of war has turned to sadness."

Soldiers were soon more frequent in Monroe County. Part of General Floyd's Confederate Army was stationed at Red Sulphur Springs for the winter. They seemed to be coming and going all the time.

There were constant rumors, many of them about Negro uprisings that caused local panic. The stories were highly exaggerated, however; some Negroes were leaving the county and some had joined the Federal troops that had passed through.

Trip was very concerned about his boys who were now in their twenties. Ralph tried to ease his concerns by telling him that many of these rumors and fears were tools that the politicians used to rouse the people to action. The fear, however, was present, so Trip and his children decided that it would be best if his sons and daughter, dressed as a man, went on to the Ohio country because sometimes Negroes were shot out of panic. His sons promised that they would send for Trip and Claire as soon as the war was over.

Trip talked it over with Mr. Smith and was assured that he had a home there for as long as he lived. His sons and daughter left one evening on horseback. They decided to travel mostly at night following the New River to the Kanawha River and into the State of Ohio, where Negroes were free.

Men were volunteering for the Confederate Army from all over the county. Henry Pyles from Lillydale joined Captain Bernie Chapman's battery of Light Artillery in April 1862, along with his father George Inyor Pyles. They fought in a battle at Pearisburg on May 10th and in the Battle of Lewisburg on May 23rd. The fact that they were in the Army less than two months and had already fought in two battles made them heroes in Lillydale.

Their neighbor J. Plucket Fisher fought with Captain Thomas A. Bryan's company of Virginia Artillery, a Monroe County unit. They served along with Chapman's battery under Major William McLaughlin's battalion.

Ralph's neighbors who had enlisted in 1862 were:
Joseph A. H. Ellison and his younger brother, J. Matthew Alexander Ellison
Joseph's brother-in-law Jacob W. Bare and his younger brother, John Henry Clay Bare
George C., Henry Lewis and Samuel Green Weikle
Henry W. Kessinger

All were in Ralph's company in the 166th Militia. They had joined Captain Lewis Addison Vawters' company that was formed in Centerville. The pressure was on Ralph, at age 37, to enlist.

With the local soldiers coming home on occasion, all the children were marching around with wooden guns. The main subject of conversation was the war.

By May, much of Greenbrier County was controlled by Federal troops and sixteen hundred Yankees had crossed the river near Alderson, passed through Union and were camping near Centerville. It wasn't long before General Loring and his 45th Regiment of Virginia Volunteers moved up from Pearisburg and ran General Crook and his Yankees all the way back through Fayetteville to Charleston.

Right in the middle of this commotion, Mary Jane had the daughter she had been hoping for, Sophronie Caroline Smith. This was their seventh child, born in the middle of a war.

It seemed like once a week someone would come by trying to talk Ralph into enlisting. He knew that he might have to go one day, but in the meantime he was trying to figure out how he could hide food and plan his family's survival if he were away. Mary Jane could run the farm and he had trained his boys well in farm work. He also helped organize the neighbors so they could look after the needs of each other.

CHAPTER ELEVEN
Ralph Joins the Army

Meanwhile, at Camp Narrows, Alexander Ellison was a wagoneer in the Army hauling supplies to all the units that were camped there. His main occupation was figuring out ways to get back to Lillydale to see his new wife, Olivia, for he had been married for less than a year.

One day on his rounds he noticed something unusual, there was a young private who had his own horse at camp. He was certain that he wasn't a carrier so he got acquainted with this private whose name was Hansbury Roles.

He asked, "How is it that you can keep a horse at camp?"

"Well my brother is Captain Christopher Roles of Company C, 36th Virginia Infantry and my other brother John Roles is in this company along with my cousins Sergeant Christopher C. Roles and J. C. Roles. My father, Mordicai Roles is elderly and is not in good health and my older brother worries about him, so we brought a horse from home so that we can go see about him whenever we can."

"How is it that you are driving a wagon? Hansbury asked.

"You see I have a bad front tooth and it is difficult for me to tear the paper off cartridges in firing drill so they assigned me to a wagon."

"By the way, I live in Monroe County at Lillydale. The next time you got to go see your father I will pay you to let me ride double with you to Indian Creek."

It wasn't long before they both had a few days off and Hansbury was going home so he gave Alexander a ride to the mouth of Indian Creek. By the time they arrived there it was raining hard. Alexander said he would pay extra if Hansbury would take him on to Lillydale and that Hansbury could spend the night and ride home the next day.

When they arrived in Lillydale they were both wet and hungry. It so happened that Alexander's wife's sister, Elizabeth, was there. It wasn't long until Hansbury and Elizabeth were highly enamored with each other. From that day on Alexander didn't have to pay Hansbury for a ride home.

The next big problem was to get Elizabeth's father, Mr. Frederick Baker, to permit Elizabeth to date a boy from outside the community, especially a Baptist soldier.

They were able to see each other at Alexander's house, but it wasn't long before Mr. Baker caught on and kept Elizabeth at home whenever Alexander was due home.

In July 1862, General Jones ordered his 36th Infantry to Salt Sulphur Springs to protect Union in the event that Federal troops should return. The Greenbrier Valley was getting more protection now as it was considered to be one of the granaries of the Confederacy.

No one was happier about the move than Private Roles, for it was only three miles to Elizabeth's house, shoot; he could walk that backwards. The big battle, of course, was Elizabeth's father.

Elizabeth enlisted her mother in persuading her father to allow her to invite Hansbury and his brothers to their home for Sunday dinner. After all, it would be a patriotic thing to do in supporting the soldiers in their effort to protect their home. Mr. Baker's inclination was to flat out decline, but being the old fox that he was,

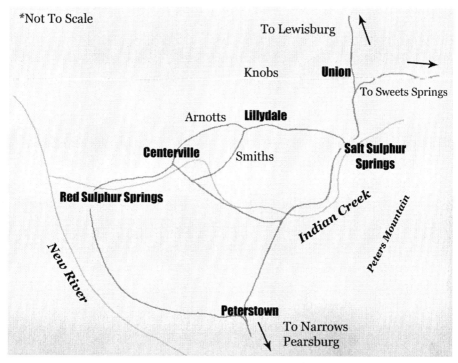

he had a scheme that would end this relationship without him looking bad in the eyes of his family. He would ask the boy right up front what his intentions were and that might scare him away.

On the way to the Bakers' house, the Roles brothers were talking it over. Obviously Mr. Baker wants to know if Hansbury is good enough for his daughter. "If I play his game I'll be under his control from now on!" Hansbury said.

Christopher said, "We'll change the tactics on him. Let's let him prove that his daughter and family are good enough for the Roles family.

Elizabeth's mother Nancy had formulated her own rules. There would be no discussion of Elizabeth and Hansbury until after the dinner when everyone was full and happy. Her cooking had changed many minds in the past.

During dinner Mr. Baker and the Roles brothers were sizing each other up like two bulls in a pen. After dinner the men retired to the front porch and Mr. Baker in his best German diplomacy said right off,

"Young man, what are your intentions toward my daughter?" Before Hansbury could open his mouth.

Christopher spoke up, "Sir, I represent this lad's father and before Hansbury answers your question, I'm sure his father would like for us to introduce ourselves. For myself."

I was a schoolteacher, a surveyor and a Sheriff in Raleigh County and now I have been entrusted to be a Captain in the Confederate Army of America. This entitles me to respect. I will now introduce our father, Mordicai Roles, who owns a fine thousand-acre farm on the mountain above Indian Mills, on which he runs one hundred fifty head of white-faced cattle. He is also a Christian and trustee of Indian Creek Baptist Church."

"Now, Sir, how many acres do you own?"

At that, Hansbury spoke up and said that he would now answer the question of his intentions.

"I would like to marry your daughter Elizabeth, do you have any objections?"

"Well," he said, "where do you intend to live?"

"I like this area and the people. If I could find a suitable farm I could live here."

"I would like for my son-in-law to live within walking distance and belong to the Methodist Church."

"I don't see much difference between one church and another as long as they worship the same God," Hansbury replied.

"Well then, I don't see any reason you can't come to see Elizabeth," he said.

Hansbury made weekly trips to the Baker home until his unit was ordered to the Kanwaha River on a Friday, August 29, 1862.

That fall near Lillydale, there was a scattered outbreak of typhoid fever for which no one knew the cause. Folks would stay at home and boil their sheets and towels every day until the disease subsided.

In December, there was talk at the store. It seems that a New York newspaper ran a story suggesting that the Federals should run the people out of Virginia and divide their land between the invaders. This struck at the hearts of the farmers and it was the last straw for Ralph. He decided to enlist. Besides, there was a rumor that the Confederate Government was about to order a conscription for all men up to the age of forty-three. If Ralph had to go, he wanted to be with his friends in Co. C, 30th Battalion of Virginia Sharp Shooters.

He would give his family a good Christmas and leave after the first of the year. It was a quiet religious event, no fireworks or joyous dinners. Instead there were prayers for loved ones' safety and when they gave thanks for the food, they really meant it. The joy of that Christmas was in being together and the homemade toys for the children.

As long as Ralph was still at home, the recruiters kept coming to see him.

One fellow told Ralph, "Joining the Army will be the high point of your life."

Ralph said, "I have already had the high point of my life and that was when my babies were born."

His answer was always the same, "I'm going to enlist when I have things in order."

Another fellow from Union came by: "One of these days the war will be over and the men who served will come home as heroes. You know you can't come back from where you have never been."

Ralph said, "Sir, you are good, that's the best one I've ever heard."

Ralph had already made up his mind to enlist on February 13th but did not give this fellow the satisfaction of telling him so.

He knew there wasn't much going on in the Army camp due to the extremely cold weather. In fact, many men had been furloughed so they could go home and get something decent to eat as the Army rations were running low.

That January, Ralph helped Mary Jane at home and made sure she had enough dry wood in to see them through the winter. He also went around to visit all the friends and neighbors to say farewell and ask them to look in on his family occasionally. It was the same battalion that many of his friends from the 166th Virginia Militia were in before they joined the active Army.

From the neighbors he learned that Michael Mann from Centerville and Jacob Bare from Salt Sulphur Springs were planning to enlist so Ralph went to see them so that they could all enlist at the same time. They would go to the Giles County Court House in Pearisburg and enlist in Captain Lewis Vawter's company.

It also was the same company that Ralph's brother, John Smith, was in before he was wounded in action at Fayetteville in 1862. He was now at home recovering.

CHAPTER TWELVE
In The Army

It was a cold, sad morning when Zack came by in his four-seat carriage to pick up Ralph for their trip to Pearisburg. Zack took them to camp, as he wanted to visit the men who had been in his unit in the militia. Jacob Bare had walked to Lillydale and they would pick up Michael Mann at Indian Creek.

They followed the turnpike to Red Sulphur Springs, over to Peterstown, and spent the night at Grey Sulphur Springs near Peterstown. The next morning, they traveled the fourteen miles on to Pearisburg following a narrow trail on the east side of New River.

On the way, Zack explained his heart condition. Doctors had told him that strenuous military conditions could kill him, so he would remain home and help with county administration of the war effort.

They arrived on Thursday afternoon and were greeted by Captain Charles Vawter and First Lieutenant Cephur Oberchain. Captain Lewis Vawter's company was up to capacity and Major Otley directed new enlistees into Company D. The two Captain Vawters were brothers and both from Centerville. Ralph was told that there were fifty men from Monroe County in Company D and that he should feel at home with them. Both of these companies were part of the 30th Battalion of Virginia.

The sharpshooters who bivouacked at Camp Success near Pearisburg. The unit was in charge of protecting the ford across New River at the Narrows, as it was one of the few places that the New River could be crossed by wagon. Whoever controlled the Narrows controlled that part of western Virginia.

After a brief orientation, the men were issued uniforms and equipment but no ammunition until they had received firearm instruction, even though Ralph had brought his own rifle musket. The issue of uniforms consisted of:

1 each slouch hat
2 each cotton shirt and drawers
1 each overcoat
1 pair leather brogans (shoes)
1 pair wool trousers
1 each Infantry short jacket with sleeve chevron and blue trim
1 pair suspenders
2 pair cotton socks
1 set brass infantry buttons

In addition to the uniforms they were issued:

1 wool blanket
1 waist belt with CSA buckle
1 cap box with open flap
1 cartridge box
1 bayonet scabbard
1 wooden canteen
1 cloth ditty bag
1 tin drinking cup
1 canvas haversack with shoulder belt
1 knife and spoon
1 oil cloth for rain

The quartermaster Sergeant said, "If you want anything else you'll have to take it off of a dead Yankee!"

The first week of camp was drilling and marching with a meal of beans and bread to look forward to at the end of the day.

Ralph had been a 3rd Sergeant in the 166th Militia but now found himself to be a private at $11.00 a month. The rank slots were filled as some of the men in the battalion had already been to Tennessee and saw action at Fort Donelson in February 1862.

The weather temperature that February seldom got above freezing, even in the daytime, so the troops were crowded into any form of housing they could find. Anyone attempting to live in tents was soon on sick call and some of them never heard from again. There was a bugle call at 6:00 a.m. followed by a roll call. They had until 7:00 a.m. to get their housing in order in time for breakfast. When weather permitted, the day was spent in drill and discipline. The goal was to get the men to act as one for the field commands given. It took a while to get a farmer to do this so they had to drill the hell out of them.

One of the best things that Ralph did was to keep the clothes that he wore to camp as he would wear them under his uniform to keep warm on cold days. He had also worn a different pair of shoes each day to insure a dry pair for the next day. After a week of marching, the new men were issued weapons that were left from men who were sent home sick or had deserted. There was an assortment of guns including about thirty shotguns. Ralph looked them over and said he would keep his own.

The entire month of March was devoted to drills. There would be days of squad drills consisting of eight soldiers working together, then company size drills controlled by voice commands. Drills had increased from twice to three times a day. They drilled from 9:00 a.m. to 10:00 a.m., then 11:00 to noon and again from 3:00 p.m. to 4:30 p.m., every day except Sunday.

The officers became concerned, as tempers were flaring among the troops from the monotony of the drilling. One day the men were excused from drill and were called to assemble. A Lieutenant, who had been wounded in action at Fayetteville and was recovering from shotgun wounds to his left arm and hand, spoke to the troops and discussed the importance of drill. He said he had seen troops who had very little drill and in some cases hadn't fired their weapons before they were rushed into action. He also said there was a tendency for untrained troops to charge and keep on charging right into an enemy trap resulting in high casualties. Often the command to retreat is just as important as the command to charge as it reduces casualties and can draw the enemy into your trap. In most cases, it is impossible for the individual soldier to know everything that is going on in the battle and unwise for them to try to predict the best course of action, so it is vital that all soldiers act as one unit. That is why there is so much drilling.

The company commander had handbooks available for training but they were of little use, as half the company could not read. Also, the book was difficult to understand by those who could read. For example:

"In oblique alignment at open order, the rear rank need not endeavor to cover their file leader since the object of this instruction is to exercise the soldier's in aligning themselves correctly in their respective ranks in every direction."

"To break up the monotony of drill, we will today execute rifle training." The Captain announced.

"About time," Ralph said to himself, for he had been in the Army for six weeks and hadn't fired a round.

The Ordnance Sergeant said, "Each man will be issued only three rounds as the Unit is short on ammo."

Ralph said, "They will need more than that just to sight the guns in." The shortage of ammunition was discouraging to the troops. The consensus of the troops was that they were going to war short on ammunition. "Why didn't the politicians think of this when they were talking up secession?"

After their first shot at a one hundred-yard target, Ralph could tell that most of the weapons were shooting low. Ralph talked to his Sergeant and offered to sight in the guns for the company. The Sergeant said he would relay it to Captain Charles Vawter. The Captain knew of Ralph's reputation as a hunter and said he would have Ralph to do it just as soon as they received a shipment of ammunition.

Time had come for them to do drills on the battalion level, but first they had to learn to receive commands by a trumpeter or drummer as voice commands couldn't be heard in a large unit, much less in the noise of battle.

Private Sylvester Ballard of Red Sulphur Springs was the company drummer and Private Madison Ballard of the same community was trumpeter and chief musician.

Many men had no ear for music and had to ask the man next to him what the sound meant.

Now that they had received a shipment of ammunition they could learn the motions of loading and firing in rank. Their objective was to have each man load, aim and fire three rounds within one minute.

Ralph had loaded and fired many a time while on the run or laying on the ground, but this time he had to do it the Army way, which was a nine-step procedure:

1. *Remove the cartridge from the box on the belt*
2. *Tear the paper end off with your teeth*
3. *Pour the powder into the barrel*
4. *Place the bullet into the barrel*
5. *Draw the rammer*
6. *Insert the small end of the rod and ram the load into the barrel*
7. *Return the rammer into its holder*
8. *Install the primer*
9. *Cock, aim and fire*

Keep practicing until the goal of three rounds per minute is obtained.

Both of the Vawter Captains had known of Ralph's abilities with guns and his Captain, Charles Vawter, told him that if he had joined in early 1862 he would be a Sergeant by now but rank had been filled with experienced men. The Captain told Ralph that he would try to find a place for him. Some men wondered if he was sincere or if he just didn't want to have to face Ralph after the war.

The Ellisons and Bare brothers, who were in Company C under Captain Lewis Vawter, told Ralph and the Weikle brothers that they were fortunate to be in Company D because Lewis Vawter had a temper that would run off a mountain lion. At times he had lost his temper with some of the men and had gotten in trouble for it with Colonel Clarke, the battalion commander.

There were some men in Ralph's company from Floyd, Grayson and Botetourt Counties and he passed his spare time talking about farming with these gentlemen. Most of the men were much younger then Ralph, who was now thirty-seven, so he tried to find the older fellows to talk with.

One day in formation they were told that there would be a marksmanship contest between companies with the three best marksmen from each company participating. Lt. Col. J. Lyle Clarke and his assistant Major Peter J. Otley would judge the contest. A range was set up and each contestant fired at targets from one hundred to four hundred yards. Ralph, of course, had been selected for Company D and he had his rifle musket well sighted-in.

After a half-day of shooting and some stiff competition, Ralph won by placing 13 out of 15 shots inside a one-foot diameter target at 400 yards.

The award was a surprise as Ralph and a man from Mercer County were selected for a special assignment. The battalion had received two British Whitworth rifle muskets with marksman scopes that ran the full length of the barrel. Colonel Clarke told the men that this rifle could take down a man from one thousand to twelve hundred yards.

The primary purpose of these rifles was to pick off the artillery crew when there was incoming cannon fire from beyond eight hundred yards.

These rifles would be kept in ordnance and signed out only by those designated to use them. It was not practical to use them in routine training as the weapon alone weighed thirty-five pounds.

They were told, "You are to select a helper and practice with these weapons until you are proficient. You will also be relieved of extra duty while you are on this assignment."

Ralph selected Private Lorenzo Halstead as his helper. Lorenzo was from Stinking Creek near New River. The teams' duties were to practice judging distance and firing at long-range targets.

In April the entire battalion, including full support of supply wagons, ordnance, commissary, surgeons, band and color guards marched to a place on New River where the bottomland was cleared and large enough to allow for a full frontal formation.

Major Peter Otley left for Wytheville and was married on April 14th. There were no plans for the battalion in his absence, so Ralph was able to get a four-day pass to go home. It was reassuring to Ralph to see that his family was doing well in spite of the shortages. Mary Jane was operating the farm the best she could with the help of her boys and Trip.

Ralph and Mary Jane did have some time together and they were happy. They both felt that the war wouldn't last long and they would be back to normal soon.

Back at camp the battalions received their first shipment of Enfield.577 rifles from England. They were rifled barrels and fired "Minnie" bullets instead of round balls. This bullet was invented by Captain Clause Etienne Minnie of the French Army and was more accurate than the round balls. When fired the round balls tended to jar around in the barrel and were less accurate than the Minnie bullet as the bullet had a hollow base, which expanded when fired to fit the grooves in the barrel. This increased the accuracy and the velocity.

That May the battalion was ordered to Smyth County, Virginia, to guard the salt mines at Saltville and to protect that section of the Virginia-Tennessee Railroad.

They traveled to Saltville by railroad, which was the first train ride that most of the men from Monroe County had ever had. They sure had something to write home about.

There were no Yankees within a hundred miles of Saltville so after a month they were ordered back to what was now Camp Clarke at the Narrows.

The first Yankees that Ralph had seen were a group of prisoners being marched to Dublin to catch a train to Richmond.

In his spare time, Ralph wrote letters home for some of the men who couldn't read or write — he wondered if there would be any one at home that could read the letters. He also conducted Sunday school classes for those in his company that could attend.

In the summer of 1863, Mary Jane had her hands full with seven children and a farm to work. Her brothers and sisters would come by when they could to help out and her father, Henry, would come by often as he loved the children.

Mary Jane tried to go to church every Sunday to pray for Ralph and to hear any news of the war from neighbors. The neighborhood now seemed to be a much closer group, as things were difficult. The preacher felt the concerns of the people and offered more hope and faith and a little less hell fire in this sermons.

One day as Mary Jane was hitching up the horses, a bee stung one of the mares and as she kicked a hoof it caught Mary Jane's left hand against the single tree. It crushed two of her smaller fingers. Since there were two doctors in Union and only one in

Centerville, she figured she would have a better chance of finding one in Union. She took the mare and rode her as fast as she could as she fought back the tears.

Dr. Douglas amputated the two fingers from the middle joint down, gave Mary Jane some morphine and put the hand in a sling. She had her fingers cut off by noon and was back on the farm working before the afternoon was over.

June 1863 was a disturbing month in Monroe County. Most of the northwest counties of Virginia had seceded from the Commonwealth and had taken Monroe, Greenbrier and Mercer counties with them without much consultation from Monroe County. A government for this new state called West Virginia had assembled in Wheeling and delegates from Monroe County were not even invited.

This caused considerable debate throughout the County and people from Lillydale headed to The Salt to find out what was going on. Mr. Sheldon said, "We are now a Yankee state and all of our men in the Confederate Army are now theoretically fighting us."

Others said, "This proves that Mr. Sheldon is just plain crazy."

"How did this happen?" they asked.

"Well, you see, the people in Richmond didn't pay much attention to the people who live across the Allegheny Mountains. They took our taxes and spent them on projects in eastern Virginia," said Mr. Wall, the storekeeper.

Mary Jane thought to herself, "If Ralph were here, he would say that it was because Richmond stopped the Virginia Central Railroad at Jackson River in 1858."

There were many meetings held in the Greenbrier Valley to get the railroad extended west, but nobody in Richmond would listen.

"So as of June 20th all slaves will become free and we will be governed from Wheeling where no one from around here has been," said Mr. Seldon.

To top off the month, Mr. William Erskine, the hotel and resort manager, died. There was a huge crowd at the church for the funeral that spilled out into the road. Most people had a high regard for him for the way that he had built The Salt. They all wondered what would happen next.

In August, Mary Jane received a letter from Ralph.

"We are deep into Tennessee, all the way to Nashville. Still no real fighting, mostly guarding the railroad and drilling. Tell my boys that I have been promoted to 2ⁿᵈ Corporal and explain to them that all corporals are the same rank and the number in front refers to my position in a battle formation. Please tell the Ellisons that Joseph and Alexander are doing well."

The 30ᵗʰ Virginia Battalion of Sharpshooters had become part of Brigadier General Gabriel's Warton Division under Major General John C. Breckinridge Corps.

"Tell the Bakers that Hansbury Roles, 36ᵗʰ Virginia Infantry, is now in our division and that I can walk over to see him now and then."

By the time Mary Jane had received his letter, Ralph had been to Staunton and then onto Winchester to support General Robert E. Lee's Army of Northern Virginia as they returned to the Valley of Virginia following the defeat in Gettysburg. They had spent a couple months in the valley doing picket duty and drilling before they were ordered back to Saltville. From there they were sent back to Tennessee. Ralph certainly enjoyed the train ride as much as he did seeing the fine farms along the way.

They spent the fall marching and drilling. Ralph wrote home again:

"Dear wife Mary Jane,

I hope this finds you well. Tell the children that I think of them all the time. I wish I could be with you. I'm sorry I joined this Army, it is such a waste of time as we are chasing ghosts down here. There aren't any Yankees anywhere and we are marching all over the country looking for them. Sometimes I wonder if the Colonel has lost his mind. We have marched back and forth until our supplies have run out. Many men are falling out sick and others are deserting cause they didn't sign up to protect Tennessee.

Men's shoes have worn out and we sleep in snow on long marches. Four men in my company had frost bite this week. Food is scarce. I've been sent out to deer hunt for food. I sure miss your cooking.

Rumors say we'll be back at Narrows by spring, but in this outfit no one knows what to expect except for drilling. The men are calling it "Clark's Military School."

Say hello to my parents and to Mr. Henry for me and kiss the children and tell them that I'll be home just as fast as I can.

I love you,

Your husband

Ralph

CHAPTER THIRTEEN
The Battle

Lillydale survived another winter with shortages. Some said it was like the pioneering days when they lived on game and chestnuts. The people had long been tired of the war and prayed for the day it would end. New laws and regulations were coming in all the time from the State of West Virginia. County officials who were pro-Richmond were now out of office and new people were appointed. Many people were torn between the two states.

All Mr. Sheldon could add was that, "We are now behind enemy lines."

Mary Jane's brother Zachariah, a Lt. Colonel, had a particularly hard winter by being sick most of the time. He had spent time with his brothers and sisters as he was not married and he needed help with food and medicine. His heart finally failed him on Thursday, March 27th, 1864. This deeply saddened Mary Jane as they were near the same age growing up. It was also hard on her father Henry, as Zachariah was the ninth member of his family to die.

Lt. Colonel Zachariah Phillips Arnott of the Monroe County's 166th Militia was well known — a popular man in county politics. He had helped train many men who were in the war. They were:

Joseph A. H. Ellison, Corporal, Co. C, 30th Virginia S.S.
J. Matthew Alexander Ellison, Pvt., Co. C, 30th Virginia S.S.

Jacob W. Bare, Pvt., Co. C, 30th Virginia S.S.
John H. C. Bare, Pvt., Co. C, 30th Virginia S.S.
Madison Ballard, Musician, Pvt., Co. D, 30th Virginia S.S.
Sylvester Ballard, Drummer, Pvt., Co. D, 30th Virginia S.S.
Green Canterbury, Pvt., Co. C, 30th Virginia S.S.
Ralph Smith, Corp., Co. D, 30th Virginia S.S.
Henry Kessinger, Pvt., Co. C, 30th Virginia S.S.
Richard E. McNeer, 2nd Lt., Co. C, 30th Virginia S.S.
Isaac Smith, Corp., Co. D 30th Virginia S.S.
Henry T. Weikle, Corp., Co. D, 30th Virginia S.S.
Samuel Green Weikle, Pvt., Co. D, 30th Virginia S.S.
Henry Pyles, Pvt., Chapman's Battery
Geo. Inyor Pyles, Pvt., Chapman's Battery
Jessie R. Arnott, Pvt., Chapman's Battery
John I. Fisher, Pvt., Bryans Battery
J. Plucket Fisher, Pvt., Bryans Battery
and many more from Monroe County.

Since these men were away in service, their fathers organized a march behind the horse drawn hearse and had a funeral procession from Union to the cemetery on the hill in Lillydale. The ones that couldn't march rode on horses or in carriages, many carrying Confederate flags. They held a military ceremony at the gravesite unlike anything that had been seen in Lillydale.

Ralph's company had arrived back at the Narrows on Tuesday, May 3rd. He was hopeful for some time off to go home. However, on Monday morning at roll call, Major Otley informed the troops that word had been received that Union Major General Franz Sigel was marching up the Valley of Virginia in a major campaign and that General Breckinridge's Army was to move with all haste to Staunton. The troops were to use the day cleaning the equipment and preparing to march through Monroe County to Jackson River Station to board a train to Staunton.

Word spread by horseback to Lillydale that the 30th Battalion was coming through Monroe County on Tuesday. Some calculated that they would likely be camping near Rock Camp on Tuesday night. Mary Jane and others loaded their children into farm wagons and headed for Rock Camp on the hopes of seeing their loved ones. After the troops had their evening meal they were given two hours to see their visitors. Mary Jane had fixed Ralph a strawberry pie, a jug of maple syrup and a poke full of ham biscuits for his trip. He held Mary Jane and their two-year-old daughter Sophronie while his boys talked with the soldiers about the Army. The men seemed tired and ragged; they were not a pleasing sight.

On the way home, Mary Jane had two boys with lanterns walk in front of the horse while she drove the four miles back home.

The next day, the troops marched through Union on their way to Sweet Springs. It was disappointing how all the stores were closed and how many of the fence rails had been burned for fuel.

At a stop for rest near Union, they heard rumors that two regiments from Ohio, under the command of Brigadier General Rutherford B. Hayes, were marching toward Union. This made the troops from Monroe County angry. After all, they had enlisted to protect their homes and here they were marching way over into Virginia when their county was subject to attack by Federal troops. They reminded both Captains Vawter that they were both from Centerville and that they may have to answer to the people from home after the war. Captain Lewis Vawter threw a fit right there in the road and started to punish his whole company for questioning his orders. Just then Major Otley came riding by and ordered the company to keep marching, as they had to be at Jackson River Station by Sunday May 8th.

Captain Vawter said,

"I'll settle with you men later."

And one of the men shouted,

"And you may get a bullet in the head before later!"

Ralph was thinking to himself, as they marched through Gap Mills, "I have never understood this way of fighting, where troops from each side would line up and fire directly into each other. I wish I had joined Thurmond's Rangers when my hunting buddy John McNeill enlisted in Captain William Thurmond's Company when it was formed at Wolf Creek. They operate contrary to all formal military tactics. They wait in hiding, hit the enemy fast and hard, and then ride off before they know what hit them. Much less chance of getting shot. The rangers operated longer than Colonel Mosby, lost fewer men, and had less press as they operated in more remote areas."

The troops were quiet and solemn as they left Monroe County at Sweet Springs. There was a feeling that they would face some tough fighting from here on. The men marched down Dunlap Creek across Humpback Bridge and were dragging by the time they reached Covington and had difficulty in walking by the time they reached the train station. The train was late in leaving the station as it took so much time to gather up the stragglers. Lt. Col. Clarke was there biting on his cigar and taking names.

Some men were so tired they hardly noticed the surroundings as they went by. They were foot sore, their guns had cut into their shoulders and their equipment had been like dead weight. If it had been August they would have never made it. The flat bed rail cars rumbled through the night past Lynchburg to Charlottesville, then over to Staunton.

Meanwhile, in Monroe County, General Crook marched his Federal Army of ten thousand men through Union, taking all the food and grain they could find. They camped that night just below Salt Sulphur Springs. The encampment extended along Turkey Creek all the way up to Willow Bend.

The Salt Sulphur Springs resort was saved, as General Crook believed that Mrs. Erskine, now the manager, to be a Union sympathizer, which she was not. The next morning was spent killing bushwhackers by firing squad. They claimed that General Crook had been shot at.

The 30th Battalion of Virginia Sharpshooters camped just north of Staunton and rested while General John C. Breckinridge assembled his Army. On Thursday, May 12th the men were issued some new clothing along with some Scotch bottom shoes that were made right there in Staunton. There were ordered to pack two days of rations and be prepared to march at daybreak on Friday.

The officers had detected a growing dissension among the men as they felt that they should know why they were up here in this part of Virginia.

They were told that intelligence had informed them that General U.S. Grant ordered General Franz Sigel to bring his Army up the valley, then turn east at New Market and drive toward General Robert E. Lee's flank near Fredericksburg.

"Our orders are to prevent Sigel from advancing toward Fredericksburg. Our cavalry, under the command of Brigadier General John D. Imboden, has been harassing and delaying Sigel's Army, which was slowly moving up the valley. General Breckinridge's Army will march down the valley until we meet Sigel's Army and stop it heads on."

Colonel John Mosby's cavalry had harassed Sigel near Winchester by attacking his wagon trains. Only Captain John H. McNeill's Rangers, who cut telegraph wires and attacked railroad trains, equaled his tactics.

The rest and extra food had the men in better spirits as they marched out of camp at sunrise on Friday, May 13th. They were marching on a macadam road on the Valley Pike which most of the men hadn't seen before, much less marched on. This caused some excitement and the men even joked as they marched.

Near Mt. Crawford, there was a rise in the road in which Ralph looked ahead, then turned to look back. He was amazed at the length of the column, it reached almost out of sight. Someone said there were four thousand men; the most Ralph had seen was nine hundred.

One fellow said, "Wait till you see Sigel's Army of eight thousand!"

Another fellow asked, "How can we fight an Army twice our size?"

Another said, "Why, I can take down six in two minutes! If the rest of you can do your share we can have them licked before noon!"

There was a large prayer meeting at the end of Friday's march led by chaplains and other speakers. Ralph had noticed a growing revival taking place, which was confirmed by the speakers.

It started to get cloudy and dark before they stopped to camp in the woods on the south side of the road. Ralph told his men to pick a high spot because they were expecting to have rain before morning, and rain it did. Most of the men were standing, leaning against trees with oilcloths and raincoats over their heads. They would just as soon march as to stand there in the rain.

There was a rhythmic sound of wet shoes hitting the hard road as they marched that Saturday morning. They began to meet citizens marching south with everything they could carry on their backs.

"We are getting away from the Yankees" they said.

"Where can we go to get away from the Yankees?" another lady asked.

An old veteran said, "You can go to heaven, there won't be any Yankees there."

The troops talked about nightmares and premonitions they were having. One dreamed of marching into heaven, another said he was driven by the devil. Another said that he had been talking to his dead loved ones and others said they had seen signs in the clouds.

The unit marched all day Saturday through heavy rain. They would spend the night at Lacy Spring, nine miles south of New

Market. That evening Brigadier General Imboden reported to General Breckinridge that General Sigel's Army had arrived at New Market and that the remainder of his Army was strung out down the valley for several miles.

Breckenridge allowed the troops to sleep until midnight then had the troops up and marching through the night and rain arriving at Shirley Hill, one mile south of New Market, at 6:00 a.m. on Sunday morning May 15, 1864.

They had breakfast in the rain and were allowed to rest while the generals convened with Brigadier General John C. Breckinridge from Kentucky and former Vice President of the United States. He was the Democratic candidate for President against Abraham Lincoln. He was a large and impressive man in the saddle as he rode among the troops.

The other generals and commanders present were Brigadier General Gabriel C. Warton, Brigadier General John Echols of Monroe County, Brigadier General John McCausland and Professor Lt. Col. Scott Shipp of Virginia Military Institute. Brigadier General Imboden and Captain John McNeill were briefing them.

General Sigel's troops were spread out down the valley all the way past Edenburg. He had about six thousand at New Market and another two thousand on the way. The Confederates had a total of forty five hundred so they decided to attack now before the full contingency of Federal troops arrived at New Market.

While the generals were detailing their plans the troops rested in preparation for battle. Ralph thought about how many men from Lillydale were there. In his battalion were:

Joseph and Alexander Ellison
Henry L. and George C. Weikle
Richard McNeer
Samuel Green Weikle
Isaac Smith

In Chapman's Artillery Battery:

J. Plucket Fisher

Henry Pyles

Jessie R. Arnott

Ralph thought, "Ten men from such a small community. I better start thinking about going into battle."

"I need to check each man's equipment and make sure they have their weem rounds in place so that they will fire a weem round every ten shots to keep the barrel clean."

He needed to review his responsibilities as a corporal and keep his men close and in line so they could communicate in the rain and noise of the battle and above all, aim to make every shot count.

By 8:30 a.m., they were ordered to set up a line of defense at Shirley Hill, hoping to draw the Federal Troops into a trap. They tried to dig rifle pits but with the heavy downpour there would be a mud hole in no time. They started to receive light rifle and cannon fire from the Feds. With incoming fire, the men took down a rail fence and built a small barricade while waiting for the enemy to charge. The Feds failed to advance so the troops were ordered to charge down the hill and set up a line at a fence at the bottom of Manor Hill. The 30th Battalion was in the front and held its position until the 51st Virginia moved in on the left and the 62nd Virginia Infantry along with two companies from the First Missouri Cavalry dismounted and wedged themselves in on the right side.

One old boy in the 30th stood up and looked to his right. His Sergeant said,

"What in the hell are you doing?" The old boy said,

"I just wanted to see what people from Missouri looked like."

As they looked over the battlefield, the humidity was rising over the soaked ground and the dampness gave the grass and trees a richer and darker shade of green. The sun was trying to break through the clouds which made the gray Confederate and Blue uniforms in the distant more brilliant.

Picture of New Market

May 15, 1864

Facing them were two Connecticut and one Ohio infantry units plus a West Virginia artillery battery. Colonel Clark said it was time to bring out the Whitworth guns against the artillery and for the riflemen to pick a target, take time to aim and squeeze off their rounds at will. Shortly General Echols formed a second line to their rear, and with that they were ordered to advance.

One fellow in Ralph's squad was awfully nervous and Ralph told him to stand still and be brave. The fellow said to him,

"If God wanted us to be brave he wouldn't have given us legs!"

The heavy rain and wet powder reduced the firepower on each side. Chapman's artillery had crossed to a hill on the east side of the Valley Pike and was bombarded by the Federal line until they retreated behind the Bushong farmhouse. At that, the Confederate line, which included the 18th, 22nd, 23rd and 26th Virginia Infantries and the VMI Corps of Cadets, charged across an open but muddy field for five hundred yards to the Bushong house and barn under rifle fire. Once at the house the line had to split to circle the house and outbuilding. Fortunately neither side bombarded the house as the Bushong family was hiding in the crawl space during the battle.

The 30th battalion regrouped in the apple orchard on the north side of the house. Just as they started to regroup, the Feds concentrated a heavy volume of fire into the orchard. Ralph was hit by a minnie bullet just above the knee in his right leg and was knocked to the ground into three inches of mud. He was covered with mud and it was still raining hard as he wrapped his belt around his leg to control the bleeding. He took his knife out to try to remove the bullet but it was too deep. He saw that the lead ball had torn through his flesh, dragging with it dirt and bits of his uniform. He couldn't get up and no one could get to him for the incoming fire above his head. He lay there for what seemed like an hour with the

pain from his leg and his head hurt from the black powder that
he had breathed. He yelled and waved his arm until he finally saw
two litter bearers struggling through the mud to get to him. They
carried him to a wagon, which took him to Smith Creek Baptist
Church. He had to wait another two hours for the surgeon to get
to him. An aide poured some ether on a rag and held it under
Ralph's nose while the doctor took a bullet (Lithotomy) scoop and
removed the bullet. It woke him up when the aide poured the dis-
infectant on the wound and applied the dressing. Some ladies of
the church worked their way around to him, took off his clothes
and wrapped him in a blanket while they boiled his clothes. After
a dose of morphine he started to get warm for the first time in two
days as he drifted into a stupor.

He was allowed to stay there on the floor over night. The moans
and piteous cries from the other wounded men woke him several
times during the night, but his fatigue caused him to go back to
sleep quickly even though his leg hurt.

By morning his leg was still hurting and he had some fever.
The doctor who had worked all night came by and tagged him to
be sent to Harrisonburg General Hospital. While he was waiting in
the assembly area for transportation, Major Otley came by with his
arm in a sling from a shot he had taken in the orchard. He asked
the men how they were and congratulated them on winning the
battle. He said that the Yankees were still on the run down the valley and that General Sigel had become so frustrated in the battle
that he started giving orders in German. He also told them that
taking good aim and the efficient use of their firepower made the
difference in the battle.

He told Ralph that two other men from Monroe County had been
wounded and that they were Corporal James Mitchell and Private Wilson Wright. Although Mitchell had a head wound, their wounds did
not appear to be serious. He had also heard that one of the Cadets,
who was a grandson of Thomas Jefferson, had been killed.

CHAPTER FOURTEEN
Hospital

Monday evening, May 16, 1864, Ralph was loaded onto a farm wagon that had "ambulance" painted in red on the side and a red cross on the tailgate. He asked the fellow next to him,

"Where are they taking us?"

"Harrisonburg Hospital I'm told."

"Long, gut shaking haul."

"Here, have a shot of brandy, you'll need it."

"Thanks."

"It took us a day and a half to march here from Harrisonburg and may take longer going back as the road is full of troops and civilians heading south."

"All they can get out of farm horses is two miles per hour for an eight hour day. That's about all these tired old horses will do."

That night the only thing they could do was sleep on their stretchers and worry about their wounds and their future.

The next day, the sun was out and it was getting warmer, which felt good. Ralph was stretching his morphine pills to make them last for the trip. His leg still hurt and he had to ask for water several times, as he felt feverish. The jarring of the wagon was hard to take and the sun heated up the foul odor from the dead animal carcasses that was permeating the air along the road. These animals had died of hunger and overwork and were just left along the road to rot.

It was Thursday noon by the time they reached the hospital and what a depressing sight. The place was crowded with patients and the noise of patients suffering gave him a sick feeling, but it had to be better than a rough wagon trip.

He was taken to a bed near a window and told that a doctor would see him soon. He soon found that not all patients were merely wounded. Many had erysipelas, pneumonia, typhoid fever and measles, and men were dying every day.

Ralph decided that his best course of action in this god awful place was to keep a good sense of humor and try to help the other troops by talking with them and reading scripture to comfort them.

Medical Report: *Thursday, May 26, 1864.*

"There is swelling, red streaks and pain in right knee, ordered lead and opium treatment."

News from the war was that General "Black Dave" had replaced General Franz Sigel Hunter and his Army was coming up the valley destroying everything in sight. General Breckinridge's Army was ordered back to Staunton and then on to Charlottesville to help General Lee south of Fredericksburg.

With the lack of food and medical staff, life in the hospital became unbearable. Ladies from the town came in to help but they were untrained. Even under these conditions, the Confederates had an advantage. The Union Army had more supplies and although they used new bandages on their patients, these new bandages were not sterile, whereas the Confederates had to reuse bandages and when they boiled them to reuse, they were then sterile.

Medical Report: *June 1, 1864.*

"Inflammation and swelling above the knee has increased, wound was lanced and large amount of pus was released, pain subsided."

The hospital diet had been reduced to salt pork and beans, as there were no vegetables available. The standing joke around the hospital was that the frying pan had killed more soldiers than bullets.

The folks in Harrisonburg were busy hiding their valuables and taking their livestock to the hills ahead of General Hunter's Army.

***Medical Report:** June 6, 1864.*

"Patient is pale with yellow hue, odor of gangrene. Rx, tincture of iodine treatment."

The Federal doctors insisted that their assistants pick off the maggots from the wounds whereas the Confederate doctors had less help so they left the maggots in the wounds. As a result, the maggots ate the dead tissue and reduced the growth of gangrene.

***Medical Report:** Tuesday, June 7, 1864.*

"Very strong odor of gangrene, patient much worse and gangrene spreading fast. Decision made to do an amputation of the thigh above the wound by circular operation. Patient placed under the influence of ether, as chloroform is not available while operation was performed. Stump was cleaned with cold water and dressed. Dispense Opium gr.i, to be repeated as necessary for rest."

The next morning Ralph felt for his leg and it was gone. He shouted,

"God damn war! How can a man farm with one leg; what will happen to my family?"

An orderly came running with more opium and Ralph spent the day in a haze. The next morning Ralph woke very hungry and was given crackers with beef tea. Ralph gazed through the window and saw a colored man with a horse and sled going around to the back of the hospital. A half an hour later he returned with a sled load of body parts. As Ralph watched, he hit a rock and a leg fell off and rolled down the hill. Ralph shouted, "That's my leg!" and more opium was issued.

A minister came to Ralph's bed and Ralph just knew that was a bad sign. He said, "But I trust I shall see thee, and we shall speak face to face. Peace be with thee. Our friends salute thee. Greet the friends by name." By then Ralph was over powered by the opium and fell into a deep sleep.

Medical Report: *Wednesday, June 8, 1864.*

"Patient had severe chills, very low pulse and difficulty breathing. Exhibited symptoms of pyemia pneumonia and died late that night. Body to be preserved with notice to next of kin." Death recorded as of Thursday, June 9, 1864.

One of the staff came in the ward and asked,

"Where's Ralph?"

A soldier said,

"He's been promoted to glory."

On Tuesday, June 14, 1864, US General Hunter's Army had reached Lexington, bombarded the east side of the town with artillery from across the river and burned the Virginia Military Institute in revenge for the Cadet's participation in the battle of New Market. They sacked the town before heading to Lynchburg to destroy the railroad tracks.

In Lynchburg, Confederate General Early's Army chased General Hunter back through Lexington all the way into the mountains of West Virginia including White Sulphur Springs and Sweet Springs. He had planned to burn the Greenbrier Hotel but had a change of mind when he thought he might be able to use it later on.

In the meantime, Ralph's body, along with other deceased soldiers, was placed in a shroud containing a preparation of:

2 pounds lime

2 pounds salt

2 pounds alum

1 pound saltpeter

Mix in 6 gallons of water

His body was then shipped to the burnt out gymnasium at Virginia Military Institute. A one-armed mortuary Sergeant and his helper saturated the shrouding with the preserving solution three times a week.

A notice was sent in June notifying Mrs. Mary Jane Smith that the body could be claimed no later than January 31, 1865. No details as to the cause of death were enclosed.

The letter, due to deteriorating war conditions, did not arrive until September 27th. The shock and lack of information was crushing to Mary Jane and all of Lillydale.

CHAPTER FIFTEEN
Mary Jane's Decision

Even in the shock of the news, Mary Jane knew that she had to bring Ralph's body home for proper burial in the cemetery on the hill. She felt that they all needed him. She had to go claim his remains even though she had never traveled outside of Monroe County.

The community was absolutely shocked when she stood up in church that Sunday morning and announced that she was going to pick up Ralph's remains.

After church that Sunday, the Smiths asked Mr. Henry Arnott to come to their house for dinner for they needed to talk. They sat on the front porch and talked for an hour about Mary Jane's astonishing announcement. Was it just an expression of emotion or would she actually go? They knew her too well. She would go. They then agreed that it would be easier to help her for she might leave in the middle of the night not prepared for the trip and they would have seven grandchildren to raise and they were in their seventies now.

They decided to show Mary Jane their support and have a general discussion about the trip. She was truly grateful for their help. She wanted to explain her reason for going. First, she and Ralph had always talked about being buried side by side on the hill above

Lillydale. She said her older boys were angered over all that had happened. James Preston had already talked about going west and he was only thirteen.

She admitted that she didn't know much about making the trip, but she had been raised on stories of her grandfather traveling all the way from New Jersey to here.

They all agreed that more information was needed and that Mr. Smith and Mr. Arnott would go to the county seat this week and make inquiries as to road conditions and the war situation as there were many Yankees roaming through the county.

In Union, they first stopped at the post office to inquire about the roads as most of the mail came through Covington. Mr. Shanklin told them that the roads, for the most part, were passable to Covington. However, US General Anerill had burned the river bridge at Covington and the railroad bridge over Cowpasture River. He also said that he didn't know the condition of the Lexington-Covington Turnpike but it was still traveled.

The gentlemen then went to the courthouse to inquire of any rules for passing through Virginia now that they were part of West Virginia. After answering several questions, the county official said they could issue passes that may get Mary Jane through Federal lines now that they were citizens of a free state and no longer part of the Confederacy.

On the way home, Mr. Smith said,

"I think Mary Jane needs experienced help on this trip. There are too many things that could go wrong. What if the wagon should break down or the horses are injured? What if either Army should take the horses, they have been doing that you know? Besides, Mary Jane only has one good hand and that much driving would be hard on her."

After a bit, Mr. Smith said, "You know Trip is talking about moving to Ohio after the war and he has never been on a long trip. I think he should take that pair of mountain mules of mine and drive the wagon for Mary Jane as he broke those mules and has been working them for five years."

"Why the mules?" Mr. Arnott asked.

"The Yankees are afraid of mean mountain mules and are much less likely to take them than horses."

"They could take that light farm wagon that I have, it will travel well on a trip and has high wheels for fording." Mr. Arnott added.

Mr. Smith; "I'll have a talk with Trip and if he agrees, I'll give him the team of mules to take to Ohio. I'll tell him I'll throw in the wagon if he will make the trip."

They were getting as excited about the trip as if they were going themselves. "We better talk with Mary Jane before we get ahead of ourselves."

Trip agreed to make the trip as long as certain things, such as supplies, were discussed with him ahead of time.

After much discussion, they all decided that Trip would drive the mules and that the three oldest boys, Henry W., age 16, James Preston, age 13 and Wilson, age 11 would go as helpers on the theory that the more in the party, the less likely they would be attacked.

Since Mary Jane's sister Elizabeth had teenage children who could watch the little ones, Mary Jane's four younger children would stay with her.

The next big question was when should they go. Two factors indicated that they should go the first of January. The first factor was the fact that the roads would likely be frozen, which meant less mud to slow them down. Secondly, the soldiers did less fighting in the winter. Many Confederate troops were sent home for the winter due to the lack of food, and the Union troops were well supplied so they could wait out the winter in camp. A third reason they didn't dwell on was that Ralph's body would likely stay frozen in January.

Trip said "What will really determine the time to go is what we need to do before the trip." After a week they finalized a list of things that should be done. Such as:

October List

1. *Cut the corn and finish harvest.*
2. *Trip will work on the wagon, install slide springs for a better ride and install a canvas top soaked in linseed oil.*
3. *Make molasses. Better figure on one quart per day plus some to barter with. Mary Jane said that one small cup of molasses per day would cut the need for bacon by one half and everyone knows that molasses will prevent typhoid fever, which is one less thing to worry about. Trip said, "We better take some for the mules. That will reduce the amount of hay that we have to travel with."*
4. *Gather and dry: acorns for German Coffee, pumpkin seeds, apples, strips of beef, raspberry leaves for tea, sassafras bark and horehound for the chills, ginseng root for barter and bribes and golden seal for medical use.*
5. *Cut and stack firewood.*
6. *Make apple butter and cider for the winter.*

Trip was worried that Mary Jane might get ahead of him on her supply list so he better do some figuring himself. After talking with Mr. Smith and Mr. Arnott, they figured about one hundred and twenty miles each way. Based on a guess of road conditions, which they expected to be poor, they figured about two miles per hour for wagon and mules for nine to ten hours per day, which calculated to eighteen days for the round trip.

Trip then figured that each mule weighed between eight and nine hundred pounds and could pull a wagon with a gross load of twelve hundred pounds. He also figured that each mule would need eight good ears of shelled corn twice a day plus at least three pounds of good hay once a day. He said that if the mules were curried twice a day and had reasonable good shelter they could get by on less. He would take a couple grazing bridles in case they found some good grass along fencerows. If they had good dry hay, free of mold, he figured between three hundred fifty and four hundred pounds for grain and hay.

To this he added his and Mary Jane's weight, which was around two hundred sixty pounds, and that they could haul a five hundred pound load providing that the boys walked on inclines and level ground. The load would reduce as they got into the trip, which would allow the boys to take turns riding to get a rest. This gave Mary Jane a weight to work with for planning supplies. Trip would have to include the tools they might need into the supplies so all in all they had some careful planning to do.

November List

1. *Plant spring wheat.*
2. *Butcher hogs and salt cure the meat.*
3. *Order two pair, well made shoes for each person on the trip. One pair to have a 3/4" sole for easier walking, plus bear grease for waterproofing.*
4. *Ten pounds of saltpeter taken from the cave on Laurel Creek.*

5. *Buy three gallons of coal oil and one gallon of alcohol for fuel. This may have to come from Raleigh County.*

6. *Modify wagon by adding an extension to make wagon bed twelve feet long in case they would have to sleep in it. Also make removable braces to prevent the wagon from rolling over on steep slopes. Make a three-inch false floor to hide guns and valuables.*

7. *Build a box to transport Ralph's remains.*

The November chores became more difficult as the Feds 45th Ohio Regiment came into Monroe County for a couple of weeks. One company commandeered Mr. Philander Kountz's house on the Lillydale road just across from the Pyles house.

Mr. Kountz, a carpenter from Keenan, moved to The Salt before the war and built a two-story log home. He later disassembled the house and moved it to a thirty-five acre farm he bought from a relative, Augustus McNeer.

The Feds issued an order that no civilians were to carry firearms. Since food was scarce, seventy year old Mr. Beckner decided to take his shot gun out to get a couple of squirrels for supper. When the Yankees saw him they shot him with no questions asked. Having wounded him they took him to their headquarters in Mr. Philander Kountz's house. That night Mr. Beckner bled to death and the next day when they removed his body there remained a bloody footprint on the pine floor.

As the Yankees roamed the countryside, it was necessary for Trip and Mary Jane to hide all their supplies including the wagon, which they took on top of the hill and covered with pine branches. It also slowed them in their preparation but they struggled on hoping that the Yankees would leave before their trip.

One cold and gloomy day, two Yankees, a corporal and a private, came riding by the store at The Salt. The store, of course, was closed but there sat Mr. Seldon by himself on the porch thinking about better times.

The private shouted to him,

"Say old man, don't you get awfully lonesome sitting there by yourself?"

Mr. Seldon replied,

"Solitude is a state of mind that affects one's reactionary tendencies and inoculates against hypersensitivities. Having suffered from acute claustrophobia in my early adolescence, I find habitation among nature's wonderments not only serene and desirous but fundamentally mandatory."

With that the corporal said,

"Come on dummy, let's ride."

December List

Mary Jane would have to make some canvas outerwear, which she would soak in turpentine for rainy days. She made a mental note to not let Trip smoke his pipe with them all, he could chew but not smoke.

Other items to pack:

Ginseng	*Leather*
Biscuit Bread	*Corn Bread*
Bacon and Ham Meat	*Sorghum Molasses*
Corn Meal	*Dried Beef*
Wheat Flour	*Dried Peas*
Dried Apples	*Salt and Pepper*
Canned Beans	*Canned Peaches*
Roasted Chestnuts	*Honey*
1 Gallon Hominy Meal	*Iron Pot*
Skillet	*Medicine Kit*

4 quarts brandy for Trip's arthritis
5 tin cups and plates for food and drink
Sundry box of knives, forks, string, needles and matches
4 gallon barrel for drinking water
Wooden buckets for mules
Vinegar as a substitute for the lack of green

Vegetables, one tablespoon per day.
For chills: horehound tea, willow bark and brandy
For cough: honey, pinesap
For fever: pepper vinegar with molasses in warm water
For sore throat: strong apple vinegar, honey, red pepper and salt
For colds: rock candy, paregoric, ginseng or golden seal, rest in wagon
For toothache: small sheet of zinc and silver coin. Acts as a galvanic battery.
For bleeding: flour
For wounds: iodine mud
For frost bite: kerosene and warm water

They would have to put items in small containers, because if people saw how much they had, they would want to clean them out, especially the trade items.

Other supplies to be taken on the trip were:

Burlap sacks to fill with hay for pillows
Rope blanket for the mules
Extra shoes for the mules
Shovel and ax
Tool chest
10 foot chain for rough lock on wagon wheels
Pick/mattock
Extra tarp for shelter
1 roll of heavy wire
1 bag of coins
1 yard of black cloth for arm bands
1 roll of twine
1 magnifying glass
1 compass
Maps
1 shot gun
1 pistol

1 raw hide whip
Gun powder and shot
1 Derringer for Mary Jane to carry on her person
1 small Bible
1 blank note book
2 pair gloves, each
1 broad brimmed hat, each
3 pair cotton socks, each
1 pair wool socks for sleeping
3 pair wool socks for Mary Jane
3 pair wool socks for Trip
2 suits of long underwear, each
1 each woolen shirt and flannel shirt
2 pair pants, each
1 wool scarf, each
A letter of introduction from Mrs. Erskine to the hotel manager at Sweet Springs
1 sun bonnet and 1 corn cob pipe for Mary Jane, to make her look old and unattractive
1 white flag of illness to fool strangers

Mary Jane even made a list for the boys to do before they left.
1. *Trim toenails to prevent wearing holes in their socks.*
2. *Wear new shoes to break them in.*
3. *Train the boys to find things in the dark if need be, so they could find things in the dark.*

Despite the talk behind Mary Jane's back about her being crazy to think about taking such a trip like this,

"It's just not a ladylike thing to do", the neighbors were more than willing to help her with the work. She asked some of them to dig a grave for Ralph before the ground became frozen and they said,

"We would be honored to do it."

The whole family insisted on everyone being together this Christmas as the possibility existed that Mary Jane may not come back from this trip. It was a quiet prayerful time. After dinner there was much discussion and it was decided that the trip should begin on Monday, January 2nd. Everything could be ready and the roads frozen by then.

New Year's Day fell on Sunday in 1865 and the church was packed with people praying for an end to this scourge called war. After church service the minister asked to speak to Mary Jane and her oldest boys. He counseled them.

"I am concerned about the impact of what you will see, you and your boys. When a person is exposed to deviation and destruction it can change impressive minds and create depression."

"I want you to know there is a way to head off this malaise of the mind and that is to pray and meditate. Take time at meals in the evening to pray and discuss what you are experiencing. This will help relieve your mind and if you feel defeated at times, pray, it is good medicine."

"God Bless you all."

That evening she took Robert Estel, age 5, Erastus P., age 4, Anderson, age 3 and Sophronie, age 2, over to her sister Elizabeth's home as they would be leaving early the next morning. It was hard for Mary Jane to leave her young children behind.

CHAPTER SIXTEEN

The Journey

Day One
Monday, January 2, 1865.

Mary Jane lit the lamp at 3:30 a.m., one and a half hours before they planned to leave. She was glad that she had prepared breakfast the night before:

Ham biscuits
Cooked apples
Blackberry jam

All she had to do now was to make oatmeal and tea.

No trouble getting the boys up as they were excited and ready to go. She just hoped they would feel the same tomorrow morning. Her nephew and his wife were going to stay in the house while they were gone to keep things from freezing and to feed the farm animals.

They pulled out of the gate at exactly 5:00 a.m., as Mary Jane felt that it was important to get a good start. Sweet Springs was twenty-four miles ahead, and if they could reach Union by daylight they would have a good chance of reaching Sweet Springs by dark.

Mary Jane had been both a mother and father to her family the past few months. Now she was a soldier on a mission. Deep down, she knew she had to make the trip to relieve her own sorrow.

She had won the battle of opinions and limitations imposed upon her by society while she was preparing for the trip. Now the next phase was to get the job done. It was a cold crisp morning. There was no wind and a bright moon as they headed for The Salt. Henry walked ten feet in front of the mules carrying a kerosene lantern and James walked behind the wagon. Wilson tucked himself in between the hay bags in the rear of the wagon to keep warm until it was time for him to walk.

Mary Jane had wrapped herself in a wool blanket and was trying to think through the supplies to make sure they were not forgetting anything important. Of course, they could use more of everything but there was just so much they could haul. There was little prospect of buying supplies along the way so the best she could hope for was reasonable shelter. She saw the outline of the McNeer house on the hill and knew they were only a half-hour from The Salt.

Uncle Trip, as the boys called him, was reining in the mules and Henry manned the brake for the steep descent down the Lillydale road to the store building. There the boys had to stop for a good drink of water as they were starting to taste the salt from the ham biscuits.

As they headed for Union along the turnpike, Mary Jane noticed that Trip was shivering and it wouldn't do to have him get sick. She gave him the wool blanket and she took the reins just as they stopped to have the boys take the lantern and check the bridge over Gin Run to make sure there weren't any breaks in the bridge deck that would injure a mule's leg. This was something they would do dozens of times. Along Indian Creek there was a long stretch until they started up the hill into the backside of the town of Union. It was starting to get daylight as they turned onto Main Street. There they could see the sign for Bell Tavern Hotel.

The boys were proud to lead the way through town even if there was only a handful of people out on this cold morning.

A cup of hot coffee would certainly be welcomed as each of them took their tin cups and followed their mother into the hotel restaurant. A mix of chicory and something else was the best they could get, but it was hot. Henry took a cup out to Uncle Trip, as colored people were not allowed in the restaurant. This was the first chance for Henry and James P. to sit down for five minutes since they left home.

They moved up Main Street and took a left between the Lynch house and the Herford house and headed up Diamond Hill and east toward Sweet Springs. One man yelled,

"You'll never see Monroe County again!" Trip said to him,

"I don't care if I ever see you again!"

They pressed on through Keenan and Mary Jane told them that Mr. Andrew Bernie, who started out buying and selling ginseng, owned much of the land along the way. Many times he had sent a thousand pounds to Philadelphia to be shipped on to China. Mary Jane took a deep breath and thought to herself, "From here on each mile is new territory for me and I can't even conceive how far it is to Lexington."

The road leveled as they approached Gap Mills. Trip said the mill and pond looked much like the one at Centerville. They were told that General Hunter's troops had cleaned out the mill and there was no grain to be had.

Soon they passed through the village and had ten more miles to Sweet Springs. The road paralleled Kitchen Creek and then stretched out along the valley with Peter's Mountain just to the right. Wilson wondered what it would be like to climb to the top of the mountain.

"I'll bet you could see the whole world from there."

There was good farmland on both sides of the road. They were having good weather and making good time but thin clouds were beginning to accumulate in the afternoon sky.

Trip saw some green grass along a rail fence and decided they better take advantage of it so he let the mules graze while they all took a rest. The boys had been walking most of the way.

The road was pretty level as they approached Sweet Springs from the west. Mary Jane watched the late afternoon shadows turn into different shades of gray on Peter's Mountain. As darkness fell, there were lights coming from the rear of The Jefferson House Hotel at the resort. They had to light a lantern before they reached the side door of the hotel.

An elderly gentleman, who introduced himself as Mr. Baker the caretaker, greeted them. He declared that they weren't prepared for guests as the Yankees had cleaned them out this past fall. Mary Jane showed him a letter from Mrs. Erskine, and he said they were more than happy to let them stay but they didn't have any food to spare. Mary Jane said that they had had a good day, and in exchange for lodging, Mr. Baker and his wife could be their guests for supper.

But first she had to establish a routine for the end of each day. She would inspect each boy's feet for problems before they developed. She would allow the boys to sleep in wool socks but they were to walk in cotton socks as they were easier on their feet. She also made them wear different shoes each day so they would start each day in dry shoes.

Mr. Baker said it would be better to build a fire in one of the cottages as to heat the hotel would require more wood than he had. It was a beautiful hotel and Mary Jane said that she would like to come back and see it in warmer weather.

Mary Jane shared some food with Mrs. Baker and they chatted while they cooked. It turned out to be a fine dinner and they all were thankful that the day had gone so well. They had their good start.

Mr. Baker drew them a map to Jackson River Station. At the station, they would have to make a decision as to whether they took the

Lexington-Covington Turnpike over the mountain or follow the James River to Buchanan, then go north to Lexington. He also told her to beware of deserters and such as they would change the signs on the road to lead people up a hollow where they would then be robbed. He drew some landmarks so they could stay on the main road and also told them that Hunter's troops had been roaming Allegheny County and had, for the most part, moved on to Salem but to watch out for stragglers.

Day Two
Tuesday, January 3, 1865

The next morning they were up before daylight with nervous energy from the thoughts of leaving Monroe County. They had not been outside the county except for a few trips taking hides to the tannery at Narrows in Giles County. Jackson River was two days ahead due east through sparsely populated territory.

By the time they finished breakfast, harnessed the mules and said goodbye to the Bakers, it was daylight enough to see across the resort lawn. Mary Jane had seen the drawings by German Artist Edward Beyer but something was different. She called to Mr. Baker and he explained that the drawing showed an identical section to the east just as this section is now.

"There were intentions to build a new section but the war interfered." Again Mary Jane offered to pay for the lodging but they would have nothing of the sort.

They said, "Just bring us news of the war on your way back."

The boys had run the hundred yards over to see the bathhouse, which was located in the center of the lawn. A beautiful building with a tiled swimming pool indoors. Coming out of the building, they could see the "Jefferson House Hotel" in its entirety. Wilson said,

"When I grow up I'm going to build a house just like it."

The wagon was out on the turnpike and rolling east as the boys ran to catch up with it. The toll collector hadn't come out to the tollbooth yet so they just drove on through. Mary Jane had a feeling that today may be different. The mules were starting out stiff so she laid a couple burlap sacks on their backs until the day warmed up a bit. A cold wind was gusting and the sky looked different this morning.

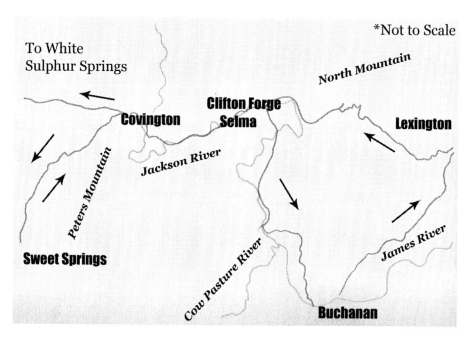

The road for the most part was level to Covington and if everything went well, they should make twenty miles today. They wanted to reach Arch Sawyers Tavern near Callaghan's by dark.

Cold shadows from Peters Mountain still covered the road as they passed a wooden marker that announced "Allegheny County" and Red Sweet Springs lay just ahead on the left side of the road.

It appeared to be vacant so they never even slowed down as Mary Jane was thinking about the day ahead. The boys, however, counted the buildings at this spring. Three long wooden buildings with long front porches; two of them were three-stories and one was two-stories. Then there were a half dozen smaller buildings and an outdoor swimming pool.

Farther down the road, the mountains seemed to be closing in as they followed the bottomland between Peter's Mountain and Dameron Mountain on the left. The scenery was changing from the blue grass of Monroe County to steep pine-covered hills.

At Snake Run where a small mountain trail came in to the turnpike, there was a man riding a mule and his wife was walking behind. They slowed down to exchange "howdies", then Mary Jane asked him,

"How is it that you are riding and your wife has to walk behind?"

"Cause she ain't got no mule." he answered.

By 11:00 a.m. the sun sneaked through the clouds and was starting to make the road a little slippery, but that was no problem as there weren't any steep hills, just a few banks to negotiate along Dunlap Creek. They had only met two groups of travelers this morning to inquire about the road ahead. The people mentioned that there were a few stragglers from the Union Army near Callaghan last night looking for food. These soldiers seemed to be more afraid of the mountain people than the locals were afraid of the soldiers.

By noon they had reached Tyger Creek that flows into Dunlap from the northeast; this meant that Hemitite was only an hour away. Because the wintertime days were short and even more so down between the mountains, Mary Jane didn't want to waste daylight by cooking a hot meal in the middle of the day so she gave them each two apple butter biscuits and all the dried pumpkin seeds they wanted. They did stop for a short time to let the mules graze on what they could find. Mary Jane called her boys together and talked with them in a serious manner. She addressed them all as gentlemen, which was something they were rarely called. Wilson asked,

"Why are you calling us gentlemen?"

"We are traveling through strange country that we know nothing about and we are going to do as an army would do. From here on each of you will be a soldier in my small army, each of you will have special responsibilities as the need arises. I am your Captain and when I say "Here", you will stop what you all are doing and pay close attention to what I tell you to do. If you don't do it then you could endanger all of our mission and us. You said you all wanted to be soldiers, so let's see if you can be soldiers on this one mission."

She continued,

"Henry will be the front scout and walk one quarter mile ahead to watch for danger and to read road markings. James P. will be the front guard and walk one hundred yards in front of the wagon and watch for signals from Henry and relay the information back to the wagon. If Henry is in trouble you are to enter the woods and come on his flank with the shotgun to protect him. Wilson will be the rear guard and watch the rear and warn us of any one approaching."

Near Moss Run they met some people with strong Irish accents, which were difficult for them to understand. Henry asked about the Arch Sawyer place but was told that it was closed and boarded up as the Yankees had cleaned him out.

It was now 4:00 p.m. and Mary Jane had to make a command decision. They had about an hour and a half of daylight left, clouds had been rolling in all afternoon, it was getting colder and bad weather was inevitable. Neighbors there told her to go two miles to an intersection with Midland Trail. Callaghan's Tavern would be one mile to the left or they could turn right to a covered bridge that would provide some shelter.

Mary Jane made a decision, she would send James Preston to run ahead and scout out Callaghan's. He was given some ginseng and Confederate money to buy a couple of simple supplies for his "sick" mother and to inquire about shelter for the night.

The wagon would move forward within sight of Midland Trail and wait for James Preston. Henry would stay with the wagon for he was the size and age where neither army would abduct him for labor.

Callaghan's was packed with ugly looking strangers and a squad of Yankees in one corner of the dining room.

Mr. Dennis O'Callaghan was busy with customers and his young teenage daughter was minding the near empty store. James Preston selected a couple of small items but the daughter would not accept Confederate money. She would take Federal coins but at half their face value. James Preston's face lit up at the site of such a pretty girl and he quietly asked her about lodging. She said her name was Megan and she was the granddaughter of Mr. Dennis O'Callaghan Sr. of Ireland, who established this tavern, and she would like to help them but it would not be safe for a lady to sleep here among all these dangerous men. She slipped him a piece of peppermint candy from under the counter and told him to come back and see her at a safer time. As he headed back to the wagon, sleet had begun to fall, but he knew that Irish smile would keep him warm all night long.

Back at the wagon, James P. reported on what he found at Callaghan's. Mary Jane was disappointed about the shelter but did remember to give James a "well done" in front of the others to acknowledge this duty. James P. told the others,

"I was so close to the Yankees that I could hear them cussing. One man said to another that you couldn't trust these mountain people, for they would shoot you before you could see them. And Megan said they are just like everyone else, except they had better clothes."

"Who's Megan?" Wilson wanted to know.

The sleet was turning to snow and the only option for shelter was Humback Covered Bridge, one mile to the east. Fortunately there was no one on the bridge. They decided to leave the mules hitched while they built a fire to cook supper in the event someone would come by. Trip covered the mules with blankets as it was drafty on the bridge. Later he would unharness and curry them, then put their harnesses back on in case they had to leave in a hurry. He didn't like for the mules to stand on the cold hard deck of the bridge all night so he, Henry and Wilson cut some pine branches to place under the mules.

After a warm meal of beans and bacon they felt pretty good considering the circumstances. The bridge was cold but dry and the running water under the bridge made a restful sound.

Henry hung ropes with pots and pans on each end of the bridge to serve as an alarm in case someone would come onto the bridge. They extinguished the lights and were almost asleep when they heard a clang at the east end of the bridge. In a flash Henry had his shotgun in the face of two Confederate soldiers; both of them had been wounded and making their way home. The lights were lit and the men looked the worse for wear. Henry made sure they were unarmed, but found a knife in one man's boot.

"I need that to eat," he said. "I'll hold that till morning," Henry told him. Mary Jane then gave them some food and they ate as if that was all they had that day.

She queried them to learn of what was ahead. She learned that the war was going poorly and that the Yankees under General Sheridan and Brig. General Custer had burned the Valley of Virginia and that food and grain were very scarce. There were roving bands of Yankees everywhere. Some Confederate cavalry units had been sent home for the winter, as there was no food for their horses.

Mary Jane apologized in advance but as a manner of security the two men would have to be tied up for the night. They protested strongly but Henry was holding the gun. She told them that she appreciated the deeds they did in the war and that she would give them some food tomorrow morning, but tonight she must protect her family. Anyway, they were dead tired, so they rolled over and fell into a deep sleep. There was about a foot opening at the bottom and top of the bridge, which created a draft, but otherwise they slept as warm as if they were sleeping in a barn.

Day Three
Wednesday, January 4, 1865

Mary Jane woke up a couple times during the night with trouble on her mind. They had traveled forty miles and it had been rather uneventful but she still had the feeling that she may have taken on more than she could handle. She was at a low point and the trip had just begun. The men's snoring brought a smile to her face so she got up and started a new day. She thought to herself, "Shucks! Ralph had marched four times this far with a nine pound rifle and a pack on his back, surely I could ride in a wagon for half that distance." The soldiers had awoken and wanted out of the ropes that were tying them up. She said,

"Hush and have a cup of Monroe County grown coffee."

The boys cleaned the bridge as Mary Jane fixed some breakfast to take with them, as she didn't want to stay on the bridge till someone else came along. The soldiers finished their coffee and said,

"God Bless you ma'am. We wish you had been with us at Winchester. With your courage we would still be fighting."

Trip was stiff the next morning and needed a shot of brandy to get him moving. About two inches of snow had fallen and it was turning colder. Mary Jane thought it was best to move away from the bridge to eat as food had a way of attracting strangers. She would wait until they found a pine-covered canopy off the road to break out the food.

The ground was frozen so the wagon moved well. So far no steep slopes to slow them down. They had been told that it was four and a half miles from the bridge to Covington, and the boys were getting anxious to see the town. Henry handsignaled James that he found something in the road. Mary Jane waved to James to see what it was and then return to the wagon. James came running back and said there was a dead man lying in the road and a dog was there with him. Trip spoke to the mules and they pulled up beside him. The old gentleman appeared to be past sixty, either that or he had had a hard life. They guessed that he had passed out during last night's storm and froze to death. Mary Jane said, "He may have been sick, don't touch him until I can think about it for a minute." Henry said, "We should bury him with stones."

"No" Mary Jane said. "He may have a family that will look for him. We'll prop him up so that he can be seen by anyone looking for him."

Wilson had already given a biscuit to the dog as he looked as if he were starved. The dog took the biscuit in one bite and returned to guard the old man. James and Wilson said, "That dog will stay here. He's about gone now." The boys wanted to take the dog with them, but their mother objected. "We don't have food to spare." Wilson said, "Let me take him to the nearest farm and we'll find a home for him." Mary Jane reluctantly allowed Wilson to take him along until they could warm him up and get some food in him. Wilson tucked the dog into the back end of the wagon with him and the dog immediately fell asleep.

They were coming into Covington now and somehow Mary Jane felt more comfortable traveling the lonesome roads then having to deal with strangers. She made it a point to avoid conversation with other travelers on the road except for information about the road ahead. She was selective in who she asked for information.

They came into town from the north and had to ford the Jackson River. As soon as they reached town, people came running out to their wagon to see if they had any food or grain for sale. It made Mary Jane nervous and it was a warning to her that the countryside was in a desperate state. She wished she had brought more food, as there was nothing to buy on the trip. James Preston and Wilson counted thirty-five houses as they passed through town.

As they left Covington on the north side of the river, Mary Jane selected an elderly couple to ask about the road and possible lodging. They were told that the road was passable and there were several muddy areas near the river, but they should be able to get through all right. If they could make it to Selma eight miles ahead, they could find several houses and barns for shelter.

They would have to ford Jackson River again as Union General Avery had destroyed the bridge. They moved along a narrow strip of land with the steep Horse Mountain on their right and Jackson River on their left. The day had been bright and breezy but dark clouds were moving in from the southwest. Trip kept looking at the river and repeating to himself, "I sure wish I had brung a fishing pole. It's been a longtime since I had a mess of fish. With food in short supply Indian Creek had pretty well been fished out. When we get in Selma remind me to buy some hooks and line as the best place to fish looks like where Cowpasture River flows into Jackson River. We should be there tomorrow."

It had been easy to find a house with a room and a barn to stay in but it cost them a half-pound of salt. Mary Jane was concerned about the supplies. With so many people around she almost forgot about the dog.

"We can turn him loose here as there are so many houses around that he can find a good home." Trip said to her, "You know, it is wolf month and we'll soon be in the mountains. There are more wolf attacks in January than any other month. Besides we are starting into full moon which is the peak of wolf attacks. We could use an extra guard from here on."

James Preston said,

"I'll set some dead fall traps to feed the dog."

I'll take care of him," Wilson added.

Mary Jane said, "If we run out of food, he'll be the first to go."

Trip and Henry would stay in the barn with the dog to guard the mules and wagon while James Preston and Wilson stayed with their mother in the house. Just before dark Trip heard some owls on Fore Mountain, which indicated falling weather. About ten o'clock that night he got up to go outside to relieve himself. The clouds were thickening and he said to himself,

"There's snow in the air and it feels like heavy snow."

Day Four
Thursday, January 5, 1865

Trip got up to look around; snow was falling.

"Today is going to be a slow day", he said to himself. He had twenty-one inches of clearance under the wagon so he could keep going in heavy snow, but it would be tiring for the mules. Better figure less than half the normal distance today.

Trip let Henry sleep a half an hour longer while he curried the mules and fed them well. He would have the two oldest boys walk a few yards ahead of the wagon to find the road and break a path. They were all out of the house and ready to go by the time Trip had the mules hitched to the wagon.

They followed the road along the river bottom south of Clifton Forge. There they saw a train for their first time. It was huge! A big steel monster with a string of wagons behind it. One car was half full of cannon balls that were made right here in Clifton Forge. The train and forge had both been damaged by Union troops and neither could be operated. No one was around so Mary Jane allowed the boys to look it over. The steam engine was like a big barrel lying on its side with a huge smokestack on top. On the front of the train was a lantern and a steel cowcatcher to push away anything that got in its way. On the rear was a house for the engineer and the fireman.

"Too bad it isn't running so we could hear it," said Wilson.

"Too bad indeed", said Mary Jane, "for if it was running we could ride it to Lexington."

While they were stopped, some travelers passed by and told them that there was heavy snow on North Mountain and that the Lexington-Covington Turnpike was snowed in, which meant the only option was to follow the James River to Buchanan then turn north to Lexington. It was the long way but they couldn't just set there hoping for the snow to melt. Frustrated, she went into a store and bought a few hooks and line for Trip while the boys explored the train.

They inched along the road and lost time crossing the Jackson River on a make shift bridge, and by early dark they found a vacant house in Iron Gate where they could spend the night. "A short day indeed."

Day Five

Friday, January 6, 1865

This day began well until the late morning sun started to melt the snow, then the road turned to mud, which doubled their travel time.

Mary Jane calculated that going by Buchanan added sixteen miles to the trip, and with the muddy road through bottomland this would take two extra days. She was thinking of ways to supplement their supplies. The boys could:

1. *Set dead traps at night for small animals*
2. *Henry or James could go to see if they could find a deer for meat*
3. *They would watch for unharvested grain*
4. *They would watch for plants that would make greens to eat*
5. *Gather walnuts, hickory nuts and chestnuts*
6. *Trip would fish in James River at the end of every day*
7. *Watch fence corners for protected grass that the horses could eat*

With any luck they could make up a day's food supply.

They also decided to get on the road at five o'clock in the morning to take advantage of the frozen road and end the day by three in the afternoon. This would give them time to hunt for food and make repairs before dark.

Day Six

Saturday, January 7, 1865

By daylight the next morning, the road had taken them into wide bottomland. They all marveled at farm fields so large and flat.

Trip said, "I sure would like to try out this new fishing pole that I cut last night."

"We'll be following the James River for the next two days and you'll get a chance before dark," Mary Jane said.

By noon, the boys had walked, run, creeped and halted to a walk again for seven hours and she could tell that monotony was setting in. Just then she saw a one-room schoolhouse and it gave her an idea. Turn this trip into a school for the boys to keep their minds occupied. She thought of ways that they could learn by asking questions not to be answered right away, but for them to study on as they walked:

How many acres are in this field?

What crops would grow best here?

Why do you think they built the canal in the river?

Would crops get to Richmond faster by canal or by wagon?

Why use the canal instead of the railroad?

As fast as the boys had an answer, their mother had another question for them.

It was getting close to the middle of the afternoon and Mary Jane hadn't seen a house for the past two hours, just flat bottomland with no shelter. Just then she saw three riders dead ahead. She pulled her bonnet down and put a corn cob pipe in her mouth to make her look older. The boys had hidden their guns and gathered in close to the wagon. The riders were Confederate cavalrymen with carbide rifles — one corporal with two privates. They stopped the wagon and wanted to know Mary Jane's business. Mary Jane had Henry show them their pass and told them that they were on their way to pick up his dead father's body.

The corporal looked at Henry,

"How old are you boy? You look old enough to be in the Army." Henry lied and said,

"I'm only fourteen." Mary Jane said,

"Don't take him away. I have seven children and I need him to help me. Besides he's afraid of guns." At that, the corporal laughed and said,

"We are looking for deserters. Have you seen any along the way?" "No sir," she said.

"What do you have to declare for the Confederacy?" he demanded.

"We're out of food, but I can give you this quart of moon-shine."

"Is it good?" one of the privates asked.

Trip said, "It is good, sir."

"Shut up old man, it may be bad."

The corporal handed it to Mary Jane and said,

"Prove that it is good by taking a drink."

She took the lid off and put the quart jar to her mouth, leaned back and took a big drink without batting an eye and handed the jar back to the corporal. He took a big swallow, leaned back and said, "Soooie! That is good!" and then passed the jar to the privates as they rode away.

The boys were smiling, afraid to laugh at their mother taking a big drink. They did tease Henry about being afraid of guns.

They came upon a farmhouse as the sun was getting low in the western sky. Mary Jane was able to negotiate lodging with a widow lady. After the mules were curried and fed, Trip took his fishing pole over to the river. Henry took the shotgun with a lead slug over to the edge of the woods to wait for a deer. Mary Jane with the help of Wilson did some cooking over a campfire and packed a breakfast of ham biscuits for tomorrow morning.

Wilson then walked over to where Trip was fishing in an elbow of the river where the current was not too fast. He had thrown a handful of oats into the river that he had scraped up from the barn that he'd stayed in the night before. As the oats floated down toward Trip, they attracted fish, and before long he had two that were eight inches long and one that was six inches. He cleaned them at the river while Wilson ran back to tell his mother to get the pan ready. She mixed a corn meal batter and they had some good eating that night.

She had noticed that Trip was awfully stiff in moving around that morning so she decided over the objections of the owner that Trip would sleep in the warm house that night. Before she turned in for the night she looked in on Trip. He had turned his bed sideways in the room and she asked him what was wrong.

"Nothing's wrong, Ms. Smith,

I always sleep with my head pointed north to align with the earth's magnetism. I also sleep on my right side so my bowels will drain right through the night. Never sleep on your back," he said,

"The weight of your food rests on your great vein and slows down your blood flow."

Day Seven
Sunday, January 8, 1865

The next morning was much like the day before; they would jar along on the frozen road until the sun turned the road into mud. They had hoped to travel fifteen miles a day but the muddy roads were holding them back. Mary Jane had a feeling that something was wrong that day, and by late morning she directed the wagon off the road to a hidden area where she cooked some food to last them for a couple days. For some reason she anticipated soldiers ahead. They had been lucky so far but they were traveling into a war and sooner or later they would run into trouble.

She told the boys to secure the wagons and to hide from sight all that they could. She even brought out the white ribbon, which indicated sickness, and tied it to the front and rear of the wagon. She would have to pull out every trick she knew to get through enemy lines. She even used charcoal on her face to make her look older. Henry was to walk with a cane and limp, the other boys would cough when anyone came near.

Each of them was given a day supply of food to carry in their pockets so they wouldn't expose the food in the wagon. Mary Jane gathered them around to pray, then they set out for come what may.

Within an hour they started up a small hill and the boys got behind the wagon to push. As they topped the hill they came face to face with Confederate troops. Mary Jane had expected Yankees but she was still concerned because any soldier can be dangerous under starvation conditions.

They were halted and an officer rode forward to investigate. Mary Jane showed him the letter and explained her mission. The Captain explained that they were expecting an attack on Salt Peter Cave at any minute and that it wouldn't be safe for them to be on the road. Against her protests, she was directed into a ravine and told to wait out the attack.

Mary Jane was more upset about losing travel time than any-thing else. Trip tried to ease her mind by telling her that the mules needed the rest.

Troops were moving around all afternoon but nothing was happening She made a couple white flags to indicate they were civilians should the Yankees break through the Confederate lines. She didn't like the position they were in because they could be seen as part of the enemy and therefore could be fired on. She would rather take her chances out in the open.

It was depressing to see the condition of the Confederate troops. This was an army that was absolutely poverty-stricken. The men's faces were ashen and bones protruded in their cheeks. Their uniforms were falling into rags and the only good part of their clothing was what they had taken off dead Yankees. In this condition, the army couldn't last long. That day Mary Jane knew that the war was over and everything that Ralph had fought for was gone — what a shame.

That afternoon the troops were strung out all around the cave setting up "quaker guns", wooden logs set up to look like cannons and scarecrows to look like troops so that they should appear to be well fortified. They desperately needed Salt Peter Cave as they were always short of gunpowder.

So far no evidence of a Federal attack. Normally they would not build campfires as they would draw cannon fire, but the Cap-tain decided to set a large number of campfires over a large area to indicate a large number of troops. He knew that most of the Yankees were raiding parties as the main army was well housed and well fed, so they could wait out the winter.

As the fires grew warmer, an old Sergeant came over to say how much he missed his children. He started to tell some stories as he did when he was home with his children. After a while Wilson asked him,

"Don't you have any stories without dead people in them?" This hit the sergeant like a slap in the face. He hadn't realized it but his mind had been on killing and getting killed so much that it was all he ever thought about. He then realized that this war would take a long time to be over in the minds of the people who had experienced it.

Mary Jane made a place in the wagon where they could take turns sleeping between shifts of being on guard. Everyone was awake and up before daylight as the soldiers said the enemy would likely attack at daylight. It was a fog-covered morning and everything was silent.

A low report was heard through the fog, the mules' ears stood up and one of them gave a low throat nicker. The Sergeant grabbed his weapon and gave a silent order for the others to be still. Everyone remained in a statue-like position for what seemed an eternity until finally a Lieutenant came slowly walking over the bank. The Sergeant asked,

"Was that a gun shot over the hill?" The Lieutenant, conscious of a lady being present, carefully selected his words before he answered.

"No, it was not a gunshot, it was Private Hill having an explosive bowel movement."

Day Eight

Monday, January 9, 1865

Mary Jane said,

"Enough! We're on our way. We will take our chances on the road." Inwardly she felt relieved, for if the soldiers had searched her wagon they would have cleaned her out.

The river whipped around like a snake on the way to Buchanan, but fortunately the road was up on the side of the hill instead of through the muddy bottomland and they were making reasonable good time.

"Yesterday put us behind, so today we need to make some distance," said Mary Jane.

She ordered the guns to be hidden as they approached the town of Buchanan in the late afternoon and it was a good thing she did for as they rolled into town a squad of Yankees filed across the road. James Preston said,

"Give me a gun, I'm going to kill me a Yankee." Mary Jane grabbed him by the collar with her bad hand and gave him a jerk.

"You open your mouth and I'll slap you into next week."

A corporal halted the wagon and checked her papers. He went to the rear of the wagon and looked in and by that time they were surrounded by a dozen more men. He said,

"You have a lot of supplies here."

"We have come along way and still have a long way to go," she said.

A Sergeant walked over to see them and said to her,

"Get down off the wagon where I can see you."

"No!" she said, "a lady does not stand around among men."

"Oh, a southern lady I see. Always wanted a southern belle," he said.

The Sergeant showed the papers to a bearded, cigar smoking officer and they talked a while as they looked at her papers and the wagon. He finally came back and said,

"You are free to go." She asked about shelter and he abruptly said,

"Everything is taken by the army. You'll have to find shelter along the way. Go now."

Trip drove on as the road was now heading northeast toward Natural Bridge. It would be dark in an hour and a half. Just a mile or so up the road they met a fellow leading a cow down out of the woods where he had been hiding her from the army.

He said, "There isn't any real shelter until Natural Bridge which is almost a day's ride ahead." He did say that there were a few barns over near the river, but for the most part they had been burnt when they burnt the Valley.

Mary Jane said to Trip as they road along,

"Something is not right here. The Sergeant let us go even without searching the wagon and did you see the way he kept looking at me? He also told us to go find shelter when he knew there was none along the way."

She thought for a while and said to Trip,

"What if they come to get us?" It was clear to both of them without saying a word. The Yankees would kill everyone of them and likely rape Mary Jane and take their wagon and supplies. "Lord, what can we do?" she asked. "First we will pray." So she called the boys together and told them what she anticipated. She then asked the boys for their ideas. They became excited and started pouring out ideas as if they were in the West.

"We'll have to ambush them or trick them," James Preston said.

Trip said,

"If we kill any of them, then the Army will have a thousand men up here looking for us and we sure can't outrun them."

James P. said,

"It is almost dark now and they are likely to come after us just after dark. It is likely that only the Sergeant and one or two others will come after us, as they will think we have stopped for the night.

Here's what we'll do. I'll build a campfire just off the road in the brush, and when they stop to look for us I'll take the pistol and scare them off. Henry can stand beside the road about a hundred yards up the road, so if they get by me he can fire on them with the shot gun while I'll come up on their rear with the pistol. The rest of you take the wagon and keep on going until we catch up with you."

By the time James Preston had the campfire built, sure enough he heard horse hooves pounding on the road. He listened and he heard only two horses. "Good", he said and hid in some pine brush beside the road. He saw the Sergeant beside the campfire looking around for the wagon. Just then James fired two shots just over his head. As the Sergeant ran back to his horse to get his carbine, James fired two more shots just over the horse's head to scare him off. But just as James had fired the second shot the horse suddenly raised his head in reaction to the first shot so the second shot went into the horse's brain. The horse instantly fell to the ground trapping the Sergeant's leg under the horse. The Sergeant yelled for the private to help him get his leg out from under the horse. At that, James P. fired at the other horse and it ran off down the road. James P. stayed still until the two soldiers hobbled off down the road looking for the other horse, then he went up the road in the dark whistling a signal to Henry. Henry nervously asked him,

"What was all the shooting down there?

Did you kill anyone?" James told him the whole story and Henry said,

"You did get yourself a Yankee, a Yankee horse!"

They staggered through the dark until they caught up with the wagon. After telling them what happened, Trip said,

"Oh Lord, they will come after us. They won't come after us in the dark. If they do come we'll be hiding in a deep pine thicket."
"We can't even see one in this dark," Mary Jane said.

"We'll just have to keep going until we get enough daylight to see one. I'll carry the lantern in front of the team and we'll keep going."

Henry volunteered. They all walked to lighten the load on the mules as they had been on the road for twenty hours.

"Trip, we are going to have to rest the mules till daylight. They just can't go any further."

At the first hint of daylight, James Preston set out on foot running, looking ahead for cover to hide the wagon. He ran back with news that there was a pine forest on the left side of the road about a mile ahead.It was about a quarter of a mile off the road on a farm trail leading near it. The boys walked ahead and found the pine grove. It offered good shelter under its canopy. The branches overhead were so thick that snow hadn't reached the ground.

Trip pulled the wagon in as far as he could and the boys cut pine branches to hide the wagon then they took some branches to drag out their tracks from the road.

They all needed some hot food to warm them up. Instead of building a fire that would draw attention, Mary Jane pulled out the can with dry sand in it and poured some alcohol over it to make a smokeless fire.

Meantime Trip had taken care of the mules. They lay down on a thick bed of pine needles as they were near exhaustion.

Trip said, "Before we leave I'll have to pour some molasses on the hay to give the mules strength to keep going,"

as he took a shot of brandy himself.

By daylight they were all asleep except the dog that was on guard.

Day Nine
Tuesday, January 10, 1865

They figured if a scouting party started looking for them they wouldn't likely be there before ten o'clock so they would get as much needed rest by staying in hiding until the middle of the afternoon.

By nine o'clock that morning the boys were taking turns with the field glasses watching the road. There was very little traffic on the road, mostly small groups of people walking.

By eleven o'clock there was a small roar, which was getting louder by the minute and it was coming from the northeast. Tension started to build when Henry said it was the Union Army. They all stayed very still as it approached. First they saw soldiers on horse in front followed by wagons. Four horses pulled each wagon and they were traveling at a fast pace. They started to count, nine, ten and fifteen total with more soldiers at the rear.

"That's it," Mary Jane said, "the troops in Buchanan were waiting for supplies before moving on. If they haven't looked for us by now, it's likely they won't. We will rest till two o'clock, then move on up the road for if we delay, our supplies will run out."

On the road Mary Jane was trying to figure out where they were from her crude map. She asked some people along the road and they told her she was about a mile from Fancy Gap and only eight miles from Lexington. Trip said it would be too hard on the mules to try to make it to Lexington after what they had been through. They decided to take it easy today and find shelter, then go into Lexington on Thursday. Another hour or so went by and they saw a farmhouse with a barn a couple hundred yards off the road.

They pulled into the road and stopped about fifty yards short of the house. Mary Jane said,

"Let me go approach the house alone. Too many people might frighten them." She looked for signs of life as she walked to the house. No smoke from the chimney, no dog barking, nothing but silence. As she opened the front gate she saw an elderly lady bending over in the garden at the side of the house. The lady was startled when she heard the gate opening but was relieved to see only a woman there.

"What's your business?" the lady called from the garden. Mary Jane answered,

"I'm looking for lodging."

The lady replied, "I have nothing, no food, not even wood for a fire."

"I'm willing to pay."

"Money's no good."

"I have food." At that the lady came out of the garden and approached Mary Jane. She had to be telling the truth, for the poor woman's hollow face showed signs that she hadn't eaten in a longtime.

"The Yankees took everything," she said.

"All my grain, my meat, livestock, even dug the turnips in my garden."

Mary Jane explained her circumstances for being there and told her that she was willing to spare some beans and corn meal. She also told her that she would have the boys gather up some dead firewood as she saw none around the house.

The lady asked one question before she said yes.

"Are you a Christian?"

"Yes, I am. I belong to the Methodist Church in Centerville, Monroe County."

The lady replied,

"Everyone who belongs to Christ belongs to everyone else who belongs to Christ. Come on in."

Mary Jane sent the boys to pick up everything they could find that would make a fire while she paid the lady in food. She also invited the lady to have dinner with them.

"Help yourself to the kitchen stove."

"Good, I'll make some bread and cook some meat as we didn't eat much yesterday."

"Oh what a wonderful day it is. I haven't had meat since November."

They all sat around after dinner and talked. Trip fed the dog and left him outside to guard the mules.

"I sure do need a dog around here." she said "but I don't have anything to feed him."

The boys reminded Mary Jane that this is still wolf month and that they had a mountain to cross on the way home.

Mary Jane thought,

"This lady is almost as starved for companionship as she is for food."

It sure was good to be able to stay in a house tonight as they had stayed in the woods last night. The lady gave her the address of her daughter-in-law in Lexington and told her that it would be a good place to stay as it was out on the edge of town.

Trip said,

"It looks like we're going to have a good freeze tonight so we should take advantage of it by getting on the road early. If the road thaws, I only expect we can do about one mile an hour and it will be hard on the mules."

Day Ten
Wednesday, January 11, 1865

The road was as rough as bark as they headed out the next morning after the wagon train had torn up the road. They were all feeling pretty good except for Trip who was worrying about the mules being tired.

"We'll have to give them a day's rest tomorrow or they will never make the trip home."

They inched along the muddy road until early afternoon, then topped a hill and there was Lexington.

"Thank God!" Trip said, "I didn't think these mules were going to make it."

They were all pretty much exhausted as they turned west on Thornhill Road to find the Moch Farm that the lady had directed them to.

There appeared a large white house with a two-story porch. "Prettiest house I've ever seen," said Henry.

Mary Jane said,

"Go on up and ask directions." So Henry went through the iron gate and started up the walk toward the house. The front door opened and a lady let out a mean dog and sicked it on Henry. He barely made it through the gate in time to slam it in the dog's face. Mary Jane was angry when she shouted to the lady,

"My husband died protecting your way of life!"

Some folks that were walking along the road directed them to the Moch Farm, which was not much better than the farmhouse they had stayed in last night. But it had a barn for the mules and wagon and just far enough out of town so people wouldn't be walking by.

Mary Jane negotiated two nights stay for a pound of salt and some ginseng.

"Tonight we will rest." There was no argument from anyone.

Day Eleven

Thursday, January 12, 1865

Sleeping late was 7:00 a.m. and Mary Jane was making a list of things to be done.

1. *She, James P. and Wilson would walk across town to Virginia Military Institute and inquire about Ralph's remains. She didn't want to expose the wagon and supplies any more than she had to.*
2. *While in town, inquire about the condition of the Lexington-Covington Turnpike*
3. *Clean all the equipment including the clothes*
4. *Bathe and put on clean clothes*
5. *Inventory the supplies*
6. *Buy a small toy for each child at home*

After a good hot breakfast, the boys were anxious to see the town. They walked east on Thornhill until it became Main Street. On the way, they admired the beautiful homes and grinned at the small barns in the back yard.

"I think they are called stable houses," Mary Jane said.

They were soon in the business section of town where the stores were. About half of the stores were closed due to the lack of merchandise. People on the street stopped them and asked if they had any food for sale. Mary Jane went into several stores until she was able to buy a small toy for each of her children she had left behind.

Their directions told them to turn left on Nelson Street for one block, then right on Latcher Street, go past the beautiful Washington College, then five blocks to Virginia Military Institute. Her first impression was that the buildings were damaged and there was no one there. She almost went into a state of panic. She ran to a couple of men standing down the street and asked desperately about the Confederate soldiers' remains. They told her to go down over the hill that they were in the burned out gymnasium.

She and the boys almost ran down the hill to the large building. They knocked on the door. No answer. Then they shouted

"Hello!" a couple of times.

No answer. Finally an old one-armed Sergeant came into view.

"What do you want?" he snarled.

"We have come for the remains of Corporal Smith's body."

He led them to a room where bags of bodies lay in a pile. The odor almost took their breath.

"He is probably in here somewhere. Give me a few days till I get some help to dig him out."

"We can't wait! Our food supply will run out."

"You have food?" he perked up. "Make me an offer of food and I'll try to help you."

Mary Jane didn't know what he expected.

"The boys can help you move the bodies and I'll see what we can spare."

"I can give you two pounds of corn meal and a pint of molasses."

"Double it and I'll find him by Saturday."

Mary Jane replied, "I'll double it but we must be on the road by 9:00 a.m. tomorrow. Have him ready and I'll throw in a quart of moonshine."

"Now you're talking," he said, "but 9:00 a.m. is too early."

"9:00 a.m. and I'll throw in five pounds of saltpeter." She said.

"You've got saltpeter? Why we need saltpeter so bad here we were going to start burying the bodies as soon as we got a hole dug. We can't preserve the bodies without saltpeter."

Mary Jane answered, "We have ten pounds but will need that to trade with on the way home."

"If the soldiers knew you had saltpeter, you would never make it home alive. I'll tell you what, give me the full ten pounds and I'll throw in a good 1861 Springfield Musket rifle captured from the enemy."

"All right," she said, "my boys and I will help you right now and will pick up the shroud tomorrow morning when I'll bring the wagon by no later than 9:00 a.m."

The Sergeant gave them masks, aprons and special gloves and told them what the tag would look like. They all started to go through the piles, moving bodies, as they needed to. After a while Mary Jane had to step out for a breath of air.

"What if we can't find his body and the Sergeant now knows what we have? What will happen to us?"

The boys were holding their emotions well but she knew that they would explode eventually, one way or another. She only hoped that she could deal with it when it happened.

To ease the tension, the Sergeant said "Look over there near the river. You can see the houses that were shelled when General "Black Dane" Hunter raided the town last June. You were fortunate to have his remains shipped here, as everything from Harrisonburg north was devastated when they burned the valley last October.

On the way back across town, Wilson said,

"I sure would like to go to a fine school like they have here." Mary Jane explained to him that most of the land and wealth were in the hands of a small percent of the population and these schools were for those families. Few of the common people have been able to send their sons here, as you not only need money, your family needs to have connections with the leading families in the Commonwealth.

"Don't spend too much of your time comparing yourself with these people as most of our unhappiness comes from comparing ourselves with others."

They met some people on the street and asked about the road conditions across the mountain on the Lexington-Covington Turnpike. They said that they would need to talk with a Mrs. Margaret Junkin Preston as she has helped many people who have come to pick up their loved ones. She lived on Washington Street near the College.

On the walk over to Washington Street, she thanked the boys for their effort in finding their father's remains. They were almost sick from the ordeal and not up to talking so they walked along silently just trying to recover.

They soon found Mrs. Preston's house and Mary Jane knocked on her front door not knowing what to expect. A lady opened the door and asked her purpose for being there in a business-like manner. Mary Jane explained that she just wanted information. The lady said that Mrs. Preston was busy helping some other folks and that if she would have a seat in the drawing room that she would be with her directly.

Mrs. Preston came in shortly, introduced herself and asked,

"How can I be of help?" Mary Jane explained that she was there to pick up her dead husband's body and that all she needed was some information. Mrs. Preston looked relieved as most of the people that came to see her were in desperate need of food or medicine.

She asked Mary Jane to join her for some tea explaining that all she had was dandelion root tea. At that Mary Jane pulled out a handkerchief from her pocket, carefully unfolding it and handing Mrs. Preston a fine ginseng root.

"Let's have some of my tea." Mrs. Preston was delighted. She said,

"It has been two years since I've had ginseng tea", and she rasped off enough for two cups and handed it back to Mary Jane.

"Keep it."

"Are you sure? Oh thank you so much. I'll make it last all winter."

Mary Jane explained her mission and wanted some advice about the return trip.

Mrs. Preston said,

"I'm amazed at your undertaking and wish you God's blessing on returning home safely."

She also said, "The latest I've heard was that the road to Covington was open but in poor condition. Just watch the weather closely and don't get caught on the mountain in a storm."

The next question was, "Where do we stay before crossing the mountain?"

She gave Mary Jane the name of a lady that had a farm in the community of Denmark, Virginia.

"Better still, let me give you a letter of introduction as many people have become weary of strangers."

"This is exactly what I need", as Mary Jane thought as she thanked her.

Mrs. Preston then changed the subject and asked if her husband was in the Battle of New Market.

"Yes, he was wounded there and died a few weeks later in Harrisonburg."

"We are proud of our cadets who fought in that battle." She said, "My husband was Colonel John Preston and he was a close friend of General Thomas "Stonewall" Jackson. My father, George Junkin, was president of Washington College until he disagreed with the politics of the Confederacy at the beginning of the war. He has since moved to Easton, Pennsylvania and has founded Lafayette College.

She went on to say that things really looked bad now that the Union Army was shelling Petersburg, trying to break the supply lines to Richmond. If Petersburg fell, so would Richmond. People from Winchester and Fredericksburg have flooded our towns. Unless things got better they may have to hitch themselves to plows this spring in order to raise beans.

Mary Jane said to her,

"I know you have a lot to do and I'm sitting here wasting your time so I'll go and prepare for our trip home." In her mind she was telling herself to get out of there before she felt sorry for the lady and offered her some food that they couldn't spare.

Mrs. Preston said before Mary Jane left,

"Light a special candle, not in memory of death but in celebration of a life and love shared."

On the way out she thought,

"Here I was at a low point in my life, picking up my dead husband's body, then having tea with the society of Virginia."

They slipped quietly back through town to their lodging and told Henry and Trip what had happened.

Day Twelve
Friday, January 13, 1865

They were up and across town before people were stirring. It was a cold clear morning and they couldn't wait to get out of town as the people made them nervous. Mary Jane said,

"There is a likely possibility that someone may try to take our food and supplies. As we leave town, we must all keep our eyes moving, watch not only the road but watch for movement in the fields on each side of the road."

Trip found a sunny spot to park and they took turns eating inside the wagon while they waited for the Sergeant.

Mary Jane's mind was on how the boys would react to having their father's body in the wagon on their trip home. They had taken it hard when they first received the news, but soon settled down to the realities of life and were coping well. Now this was like reopening a wound and it could cause many different reactions. She reminded herself of what her family, friends and minister had told her to watch out for: shock, anger, sadness and even guilt. They had to experience grief in their own way. To deny grief would be unhealthy. She had to recognize these signals and try to deal with each boy to the best of her ability.

Wilson said, "Here come the Sergeant down the street now."

Henry and Trip unloaded the box and prepared it to receive the body. The bag was still wet with the solution, which the Sergeant said was good.

"Try to keep it frozen," he said, "Keep it cold and you'll make it home alright."

Mary Jane was a bit irritated that he was talking like it was a side of beef. She held her tongue, as she needed some advice from the Sergeant about getting out of town safely.

"Wear your black arm bands and don't let a crowd gather around the wagon. If they do, show your gun and just keep moving. Here, take another rifle as I have more guns than ammunition. Hold on a while."

He went back into the building and brought out a sack. He handed her a bayonet sword and told her to protect herself. She had been generous to him. He opened another bag and gave each one of them a uniform belt buckle with CSA on it, except for the one he gave Wilson. It had SNY on it.

The Sergeant said, "SNY stands for "State of New York" but we all know it means "Snot Nosed Yankee". Now get as far as you can out of town before dark."

There were a few people out that frosty morning as they passed the schools and turned right onto Washington Street which within two blocks lead into Nelson Street West as they headed out of town.

They noticed a few people watching them as Nelson Street became the Midland Trail. They met a couple wagons hauling firewood into town so they figured that they had gotten out of town all right.

About two miles out of town they found three men standing in the road ahead of them. Where did they come from? Could they have gotten around us?

The largest man of the three stepped forward in front of the mules and brought them to a halt by grabbing their reins. The other two men started around the side of the wagon.

Trip pulled out his rawhide whip, leaned forward and cracked the whip against the top of the man's head. He dropped like a stuck hog! The mules bolted forward in a run, right over top of the man. With that, Henry and James Preston hit the other two men right behind the knees with sticks, which caused them to drop to the ground.

The boys took off running after the wagon. Trip was able to slow the mules down about a hundred yards up the road and Mary Jane looked back and saw the two smaller men lifting the big man to his feet.

"Thank the Lord we didn't kill him."

For the next five miles, Mary Jane had the boys walk in front of the wagon and beg for food to indicate to the people that there was no food on the wagon.

It was past one o'clock in the afternoon when they found Kerr Creek, a small stream that turned and twisted its way over flat rocks in a pasture field. To their left, two twin mountain peaks that were labeled on the map as Big House and Little House Mountains. They rose out of the valley floor as if they were two islands just off the massive North Mountain that was directly ahead.

"This is such a beautiful place, let's eat and rest here."

After they had their food, they all dropped their heads in prayer to thank the Lord for letting them pick up Ralph's remains and for helping them escape Lexington without loss.

Just a mile up the road they came upon the shell of an old mill but there was nothing left to be claimed. Mary Jane said,

"It's less than four miles to Denmark, let's be on our way so that we can rest up to climb the mountain tomorrow. Let's just hope that the weather holds out."

An elderly gentleman who had seen them coming stopped them for a moment to ask about the war news. Mary Jane told him that she had heard that the Yankees were shelling the railroad yards at Petersburg.

He said, "It won't be long now. Every night my wife and I pray for the end of the war."

He inquired about their mission. Mary Jane replied and also told him that she had a letter of introduction from Mrs. Preston to Mrs. Sandahl for lodging.

"A fine lady that Mrs. Preston. The Sandahl farm is up the first road to the left, past the store building in Denmark."

Wilson asked, "Is that snow on the mountain ahead?"

"No, that's Hoar Frost, clouds frozen to the tree tops."

There was a noticeable chill in the air by the time they reached Mrs. Sandahl's house. As they drove up to her house, Trip was looking around for a blacksmith shop, as an iron rim on one of the wagon wheels was wearing thin.

Mary Jane went alone to the front door and knocked. Knocked a little louder and then saw a curtain move. She waited and finally the door opened a few inches and a lady said,

"We have no food or anything else."

Mary Jane handed her the letter from Mrs. Preston. She opened the door a little wider and said, "I still don't have any food. We have enough food for supper if you want to join us."

Mary Jane explained their mission and asked for lodging and told her that they would compensate her with some food.

Mrs. Sandahl asked her to step inside out of the cold and explained to her that both her husband and son had been killed in the war and the Federal troops had taken all of her food and livestock. She was just trying to make it through the winter on roots and greens. They quickly came to terms on lodging and use of the blacksmith shop.

Mary Jane said she had a crock of beans in the wagon that had been soaking most of the day and some bacon to go with it. The two ladies got busy in the kitchen and had some ginseng tea with honey while they waited for the beans to cook.

Trip and the boys went to work in the blacksmith shop. They built a fire and Wilson's job was to keep the bellows going, which he was glad to accept as the fire would keep him warm. Trip and Henry had taken the bad wheel off the wagon while James Preston carried water from the creek. They found a few scraps of iron in the shop and placed them in the fire. Wilson worked the bellows with expertise as he had done so at home. Trip placed the rim in the glowing coals and when it was glowing red, hung it on the anvil. He welded the scrapes into the rim with a clang-a-lang-lang from the hammer. Then they fitted the rim onto the wheel while it was hot, with a few taps from the hammer to make it fit just right.

Instantly they dipped the wheel into cold water to tighten the rim to the wheel.

With the wheel back on they were able to get the wagon into the shed of the barn just as it was getting dark. Mary Jane stepped out and told them to wash up as the beans were almost ready.

Mrs. Sandahl was delighted to have food and company. She had been alone for a long time. She said things were the worst they had been since Denmark was first settled. She told them that Indians had killed all the first settlers, but the second group had been able to survive.

After supper when they were all full and warm, the conversation got around to the next day's crossing of North Mountain.

Mrs. Sandahl told them that they should leave no later than 5:00 a.m. because they should be near the top of the mountain before the ground thawed out and got slick. Otherwise it would be difficult to get the wagon up the side of the mountain. They also should stop before they reached the crest and change into dry clothes and put a blanket on the mules because the wind at the top and on the northside of the mountain would surely give them a chill. From the top it would be mostly downhill for ten miles until they reached Lucy Selma Furnace and she didn't recall any houses along the way, mostly forest.

After they went to bed, Mary Jane tried to assess how the boys were doing emotionally since they had picked up their father. Wilson had talked more about the younger children at home than he had the entire trip. Henry was acting maturer and hadn't shown any emotion at all. James Preston was able to release some of his high spirits in the attack this morning but was still hard to figure. Since killing the horse he had been running a little scared, not knowing how much trouble he might be in.

Day Thirteen
Saturday, January 14, 1865

Mrs. Sandahl was up and in the kitchen before Mary Jane was awake. As soon as she heard the pots and pans she had the boys up to get ready to travel. She then went to the kitchen to help with the cornmeal mush with grease from last night's bacon poured on it.

Trip fed the mules and left them to eat while he found his way to the house through the dark. They had a breakfast of pan-fried mush and some hot raspberry leaf tea and they were ready to travel. They all thanked Mrs. Sandahl as they left in the dark with Henry carrying a lantern in front of the wagon.

Past Denmark they were told that it was two and a half miles to the foot of the mountain and another mile to the top. The road was frozen and they were making reasonably good time considering that the grade was getting steeper. They were all off the wagon walking; even Trip was walking beside the mules as he drove.

As they started up the mountain, the road went up sideways with a sharp switchback turn as if a cow lay off the road. The sun was bright as it came up from the east, but looking ahead up the mountain they saw clouds moving in. Their breath was steaming as the sun came up but everyone was in good spirits, except for James Preston who seemed a little fussy. Maybe he was just getting tired or maybe catching a cold. In the turns they all had to push the wagon up and around the turns. James P. became impatient and started to sprinkle the mules with a handful of gravel to make them pull harder.

Mary Jane had been nervous about the condition of the mules and when she saw what James Preston was doing, she grabbed him by the collar and pulled him aside. She said,

"If these mules go down on us we could all die on this mountain, especially with snow coming."

She said to him "You've talked about becoming a soldier. Let's see if you have what it takes to be a soldier. Our mission is to get this wagon over the mountain and your orders are to lighten the load. You will carry the iron kettle and iron frying pan strapped across your shoulders and you will carry a bucket in each hand until we reach the top of the mountain. That's about the weight your father carried on long marches."

"That's not fair!" he shouted.

"Nothing is fair in the Army. You will do as you're told and keep your mouth shut about it! If you complain, your brothers will have to carry a load in addition to pushing the wagon, and then you'll have to deal with them later. If you complete your assignment, your father will be proud of you. Should you fail, then you will have to sit up with him tonight and explain yourself."

As they struggled up the mountain Mary Jane was silent. She'd had some doubts about getting everyone home safely, but was more concerned about being both a mother and father to teenage boys who could turn rebellious at anytime. At the next stop for rest she walked away from the wagon and looked out across the forest. She said a silent prayer for she did not want the others to know of her doubts.

Their clothes were wet from the effort of climbing to the top. Near the top of the mountain Mary Jane had them all change to dry clothes and bring out their wet weather clothes to break the wind while Trip prepared the team.

It was just a few yards to the summit and they could see the dark clouds building in the north. The wind was whipping through the leafless trees.

"When we reach the top we want to keep going so we can stay out of the strong winds. So let's tie some ropes on the side and rear of the wagon to keep it from running up on the mules as we head on down the other side. Henry, you sit beside Trip and man the brake."

The wind almost took their breath at the top, but Trip kept the wagon moving on down the other side. Henry ran and jumped on the wagon seat to man the break but the wagon kept pushing the mules. Trip said,

"Break out the rough lock chain and we'll put it on the upper rear wheel."

With Henry on the hand brake, the boys pulling back on the ropes and the chain locked wheel cutting a grove in the road, they were able to navigate the steepest area.

To the north they faced right into Mill Mountain as they worked their way down the slope to the southwest. The road was rocky and rough from the lack of maintenance. It was still eight miles to the next house and a light fine snow was beginning to fall. There were several washouts in the road, some four feet wide and one foot deep. If the boys thought they were going to get to ride down the mountain they were mistaken. They were kept busy rolling rocks into the washouts to keep the wagon moving. Trip even had to lead the mules across several places.

"If we get stuck on this mountain they won't be able to thaw us out till spring." He said.

Wilson said, "It sure is spooky in these woods. I wonder where the wolves are?

There is complete stillness and not a sound anywhere. Just wait till dark and then they will come and get us."

The Lexington-Covington Turnpike was originally sixteen feet wide on North Mountain, and with the washouts it was barely eight feet wide in some places. Anybody with good sense wouldn't start up this mountain when it was snowing,

By four in the afternoon with a heavy forecast it was already starting to get dark. Henry was leading the way with a lantern.

"Bring the dog," (they hadn't named him yet, just dog) "around to the rear of the wagon." Wilson said. "Just in case a wolf slips up on us."

It was completely dark and getting colder when they saw a light ahead.

It must be the tavern, they thought. "We must be careful. Henry, you go ahead alone and see what you can find out." His mother said.

He carefully approached the building and looked through the window. He saw a bar room and a lot of rough looking men inside drinking. He dared not walk right in so he waited around the side until a woman stepped out the side door to throw away some dishwater. He startled her, but she listened to his story of having his dead father out in the wagon and needing shelter for the night.

She said, "It won't be safe here, they'll rob you blind!"

"Well I guess I better just keep on going."

"Wait! There's a church about a mile down the road. It hasn't been used for a couple of years and I'm sure you won't have any trouble getting in to it. Go one mile and turn left on the first road. It's about a quarter of a mile off this road."

Henry thanked her and disappeared into the dark.

Mary Jane said, "We'll have to be careful."

"We must hurry as our hands and feet are numb." Henry led the way by lantern and James Preston followed the wagon with the shotgun.

Trip said to Mary Jane, "Forgive me but we are going to have to take the mules into the church for they could die outside in this weather."

Trip pulled the wagon around to the upper side of the church where they could see it through the side windows. Then he walked the mules into the church, right through the front door.

"God forgive us," said Mary Jane, "but we are desperate."

The first thing they looked for was a stove but it had gone to the war effort months ago.

"Bring in the alcohol can to warm us up some until I can think of something else. Boys, find some rocks to build a fire on some dead limbs. We have to get ourselves warm fast."

Within a half-hour they had a fire going. Enough to take the chill off in the church.

"We'll never get this place warm but we can survive."

They hadn't had much food that day so Mary Jane fried up some stuff in the skillet. The water in the wagon was frozen so they opened the jug of honey mead that they were saving to trade.

"I'm afraid I've been too generous with our food and we may have to ration from here on in unless you can find some game."

First she passed around a bottle of vinegar for each to take two tablespoons to compensate for the lack of green vegetables in their diet. She also insisted on checking their hands and feet for frostbite.

At about midnight the dog woke them up with his barking and running from window to window. Henry grabbed his coat and shotgun and rushed outside to see some wolves trying to get into the wagon.

Mary Jane said, "I didn't leave any food in the wagon."

Trip said, "They won't eat hay or grain, so they must be after Ralph's remains."

"I'll go outside and beat them off while the rest of you bring the box inside."

Out they went.

Once the box was inside, Mary Jane said, "This is a church and we'll have to have a prayer service," She led them off with a prayer and asked each of them to express their feelings. This seemed to be a good release for all of them.

It was one of those nights that if your face was to the fire then your rear end would freeze.

Day Fourteen

Sunday, January 5, 1865

The storm had passed during the night. It was a bright day with the wind gusts blowing loose snow around.

Wilson said, "It's Sunday and we are the first people in church."

James said to him, "You want a star for it?"

Mary Jane then said, "Let's get our mess cleaned up and be on the road before those drunks at the tavern get up."

There was a frozen, crunchy sound under foot and they had to move around to keep warm. Henry took the brake position as Mary Jane, James P. and Wilson covered themselves up in the wagon until the sun started to warm up. They would be at the bottom of the mountain soon, and then the road would be across open bottomland. Unless they hit mud, they should be in Selma by mid-afternoon.

They were not more than three miles out that morning when Trip saw something in the road. It looked like a man. They pulled over and James P. hopped out to see what it was, and sure enough it was a dead Confederate soldier, frozen stiff. "He must have frozen to death in the storm last night," Mary Jane said.

"That could of happened to us if we hadn't found shelter."

"What are we going to do with him? We can't bury him, the ground's too frozen."

"I'm sure he has a family. Let's lean him up against a tree and someone may know him and tell his family."

"Let's take him to the next main intersection. He'll have a better chance of being seen there."

James Preston didn't think much of hauling the frozen body on the tailgate of the wagon so he got out and walked.

By noon they were back to the intersection where the road divided and went south to Buchanan. They carried the body and set him up at the intersection of the road and left him there. They all didn't feel so well after that experience.

It wasn't long before Wilson shouted,

"There are the trains" and this took their minds off the dead Confederate. They said they would all come over and ride on the train someday.

"We better stay in Selma as I don't remember any places to stay between here and Covington and nine miles further on."

Fortunately, they were able to stay at the same place they stayed before. The people were anxious to hear news from the war. Henry made the remark that he hadn't seen a single deer all the way cross the mountain. They said that with food so scarce the hunters had cleaned out all the game all the way back to Warm Springs Mountain. The county had ordered food from everywhere and was now getting a few wagonloads from up in West Virginia.

Day Fifteen
Monday, January 16, 1865

They were glad to be heading back to Monroe County the next morning. Their next hurdle was to get across Jackson River at Island Ford. They kept watching to see if the river was up but it didn't appear to be as the snow hadn't melted. The crossing was tremulous, and once on the other side Trip was out drying off the mules' legs and underside to prevent shock. He also gave the mules a little hay with molasses on it to energize them.

They passed through Covington by early afternoon. Several people came out and asked for food and news of the war but they kept moving, for to stop would draw a crowd. Henry sat inside the wagon with the shot gun just in case they were overrun. They lumbered through town and back across Jackson River just north of town.

"With luck, we can reach Dunlap Creek by dark and find shelter there," Mary Jane assured them.

Trip said, "Keep an eye out for a place for the mules to graze as we are about out of grain. Better still, look for a good chestnut tree. We'll shell the chestnuts and feed them to the mules as grain."

"Good idea, said Mary Jane, "we can roast some to eat when we run out of food."

Trip laughed and said, "I heard about a woman who said she would rather have a chestnut tree than a husband for it would provide better for the family than a husband could."

Humpback Bridge was in sight and Mary Jane mentioned to Trip,

"We are on the Midland Trail, follow this road straight ahead and it will take you to Ohio."

"I think I'll wait for warmer weather."

It was 3:30 p.m. when they crossed the bridge and James Preston was excited. "I want to run ahead to Callaghan's. I'll catch up with you in a little while."

Mary Jane handed him some coins and said,

"Don't buy anything except food or grain."

James P. was all muddy and unwashed but went into the store and asked the lady if he could buy some food.

"What are you going to pay for it with?"

"U.S. silver coins."

"In that case we have a pan of corn bread left over from breakfast, no eggs or meat."

"I'll take it."

"That will be five dollars."

"By the way, may I speak to Megan?"

"Who are you?" she asked.

"I'm James Preston Smith and I have just picked up my father's remains from the war and am taking him back to Monroe County for burial."

About that time Megan came into the store and smiled at James P.

Megan's mother said, "I'm not going to let my daughter get mixed up with a boy. There are too many fine gentlemen passing through here. Go now son."

James P. fought back his tears as he ran to catch up with the wagon. This hurt more than anything else that happened on the trip. Mary Jane saw that James P. had been crying and he told her what had happened. She wanted to fuss at him for paying too much for the corn bread, but figured that he didn't need that right now. She said to him,

"People are just like that," recalling the knifing the ladies did at The Salt Resort.

"None of the people that I know are like that, and I'm not going to leave Monroe County," he said.

"I do believe this trip has been sobering to that boy," Trip said.

Mary Jane said, "Houses are scarce along this road and the few cabins that we see are too small for extra people. Besides we don't have much to bargain with. We better ask for the next barn we come to."

Day Sixteen
Tuesday, January 17, 1865

It was good to get on the road after a cold night in that barn. They were well past Crows before the sun came over Peter's Mountain. The wagon was rolling well and they would be in Sweet Springs by early afternoon. Mary Jane thought about it.

"We better not stay for the night at the resort. That would mean twenty four miles to go tomorrow and that's too much for the mules without grain."

"If we could be through Sweet Springs by 1:00 p.m., that would give us five hours till 6:00 p.m., and at two miles per hour we could make it to Gap Mills if all goes well."

They did stop at the hotel for a few minutes to see the Bakers as they promised. After a short rest they were on the road again.

"Oh, it's so grand to be back in Monroe County. Nothing can stop us now," Mary Jane said.

"Nothing but that snow storm ahead. See those clouds coming up along Peter's Mountain?" Trip replied.

"We are about four miles past Sweet Springs and if we can make it to Gap Mills, I'm sure we can find shelter there."

"We'll try, but the road is getting muddy."

"Then we'll go until it starts to snow, then we'll find a place."

Wilson shouted, "There's a rider on a tall horse coming up behind us!"

Trip pulled over to the side to let him pass. He introduced himself as William Dunbar of Gap Mills.

"There's a bad snow storm coming and they usually ride right up Peter's Mountain."

Mary Jane, being back in Monroe County, spoke more freely and explained what they were doing.

"You say your husband was wounded in the Battle of New Market? Why my son, Robert H. Dunbar, was in that battle with the

22nd Virginia Infantry. I wonder if your husband knew my son? Do you have a place to stay?" he asked.

"No, not yet."

"Well, you just follow me. My place is about a mile out of Gap Mills on the Zenith Road. My wife and I will be glad to have your company."

"We have no food," She said.

"Don't worry about that, we have food that no Yankee could find. We have plenty of room as our children are gone and we have a good barn for your team but we better hurry. I'll lead the way."

The boys jumped off the wagon to make it lighter so the mules could keep up. The mules could sense the snow so they walked as if they had new energy.

The snow was light for the first couple hours, but by the time they reached Gap Mills they couldn't see very far ahead of them.

"Only a little ways more to my house. Just follow me," Mr. Dunbar said.

It was dark by the time they arrived at the house and barn. "I'll tell Mrs. Dunbar I've brought company then come out to the barn to help you." He shared some hay and grain with them and they put the mules away for the night.

When they all went into the house, Mrs. Dunbar had a pot of potatoes and parsnips on the stove and shoulder meat in the frying pan. They were received as if they were family.

"Here's a couple rooms for you, put your things in there, then come on down for a cup of hot cider," Mrs. Dunbar said.

After a good hot meal they all sat down by the fire to talk. They were so anxious to hear the news from the war. Mary Jane told them all that she knew, and from what she could tell the war would be over soon.

"Thank God!" Mrs. Dunbar said, "Not only is our daughter Anesth's husband, Melville Tabott, somewhere near Richmond, we haven't heard from either one of them for a long time."

"No mail is coming through anywhere," Mary Jane sympathized with her.

They looked out before bedtime and the snow was coming down very hard. "Might as well sleep late tomorrow morning as we aren't going anywhere." The boys smiled in agreement.

Mary Jane fretted that they were an imposition to them. Mrs. Dunbar said, "We look forward to talking with you again tomorrow."

Day Seventeen
Wednesday, January 18, 1865

By the time they were all up the next morning, Mrs. Dunbar had corn mush and fried apples cooking. Everyone was moving rather slowly this morning and Mary Jane kept looking out to see if the road was open, but no one had passed by.

Trip went out to feed the mules and the boys shoveled the driveway. By noon only one horse had passed the house. Trip told Mary Jane, "The mules will wear out before they get to Keenan if they have to break snow and pull the wagon. Best wait for the road to open."

The Dunbars were delighted that they were staying over, as they would have someone to talk with. In the afternoon, Mary Jane told the Dunbars all the details of their trip. She said,

"Every time we were in trouble God seemed to have looked out for us."

Mr. Dunbar brought out a checkerboard and they all seemed to relax for the first time in two weeks. By the middle of the afternoon they had seen several riders and a wagon pass the house. That was good news especially for Mary Jane as she couldn't wait to see her children again.

Mrs. Dunbar told her that they had eleven children, and all of them were married and had left home and they missed them so much. Mr. Dunbar said they were members of the Carmel Church in Gap Mills and that he and his older brother John were elders of the church.

Mrs. Dunbar said, "My father, Fielden Jarvis, was a strong member of the Whig Party. I'll bet you didn't know that Mrs. Jane Erskine of The Salt as well as the Carpertons in Union were also Whigs." They talked on and on till bedtime.

Day Eighteen
Thursday, January 19, 1865

They were all up early the next morning, their clothes were dry and the boys had applied a heavy coat of bear grease on their shoes to keep them dry, so they were ready to go home.

They all thanked the Dunbars. Mary Jane tried to pay them, but they wouldn't accept anything but a promise to come and see them after the war.

The road back down to Gap Mills was slow, but once on the main road to Union they rolled right along.

After yesterday's rest they all felt good. Mary Jane was in a good mood and said,

"Your father is happy that we are bringing him home to rest in Lillydale. Let's sing a little song." And they all joined in.

"We'll jump into the wagon
And all take a ride
Wait for a wagon
Wait for a wagon
Wait for a wagon
And we'll all take a ride."

As the day wore on, several people were on the road, some on horseback. They would ride beside them and talk to them, then ride on ahead.

By the time they passed Keenan, word had spread about their arrival, and at the top of Diamond Hill there were about twenty people to escort them into Union. They noticed that men had removed their hats and were standing at attention as they rode down Main Street. Some offered food and drink, hoping to hear news of the war.

She stopped the wagon for about twenty minutes to rest and talk with people. They formed a line to look into the back of the wagon. Some people even invited them to stay over in Union, but Mary Jane said she had to go home to her children.

Several young boys were on hand as school had been suspended for the war. About a dozen people escorted Mary Jane and the boys home.

As the news reached The Salt, some people were on the store porch and waved to them as they rode by. Others went ahead of them down the Lillydale Road to make sure it was open.

By the time they arrived in Lillydale, Mary Jane's sister had her children ready and was taking them home to meet their mother. Others had rounded up some food and all the neighbors came to see them home.

Mary Jane gathered Robert Estil, Erastus P., Anderson P. and Sophronie around her, gave them all a hug and then the toys she brought from Lexington.

Before supper they all stood and said a prayer for their safe return, then had a glorious evening.

Burial arrangements were made for Saturday afternoon, January 21, 1865. It seemed appropriate that the same wagon that brought Ralph home would be used to carry him to the cemetery on the hill.

It was an overcast day with patches of snow still on the ground. The crowd was so large that when Mary Jane and the wagon arrived, there were people standing outside the fence in the snow.

The minister, in his best voice, tried to reach as many people as he could.

"Don't let our memories prevent you from enjoying the fullness of life."

"Life is full of hurtful events, especially the horrors of war that we have all suffered."

"God forgive us and the people who have hurt us."

"Let go of all those memories, unload the burdens. We can't live a full life carrying baggage through the journey that is life."
Psalms 25:4
"Show me the way, O' Lord; teach me thy path."

The Preacher said, "Put all those bad memories, regrets, disturbing thoughts, guilt, and disappointments in the hands of God and go on with your lives."

"Let not your heart be troubled for you cannot grow when your heart is filled with the baggage of trouble."

"Those who have hurt us will continue to hurt us, only if we permit them to do so by harboring those past memories."

A wounded soldier played "Amazing Grace" on a trumpet as they lowered Ralph's body into the ground.

Mary Jane had won her war.

EPILOGUE

Mary Jane raised her seven children by herself and operated the farm until her death in 1914. Whenever she had a photo made, she would cover the hand that was missing fingers with a handkerchief.

Lillydale, with a population of less than one hundred people, gained a church and a school. It also had a post office and a store operated by Elbert Roles. The community produced many fine citizens including three head sheriffs, Robert Estil Smith, Mary Jane's son, Estil Thomas and Bernie Ellison; a medical doctor, James E. Roles; one county prosecuting attorney, Forrest Roles, who was elected to the same office for thirty-six continuous years; one County Superintendent of Schools, Tippet Weikle; several school teachers including Harry Ellison and Malcolm Weikle; one U.S. Army Air Force pilot, Lieutenant Samuel Ralph Smith

Jr., (pictured) who was a great grandson of Mary Jane and Ralph Smith. Lt. Smith was killed eighty years after his great grandfather Ralph died in the Civil War. Lt. Smith died when a plane he was testing exploded over New Guinea during World War II.

Storyteller Joe B. Roles was born in Union, Monroe County, West Virginia and lived at Salt Sulphur Springs. Joe also graduated from Concord College now university.

Mary Jane's War

Mary Jane's husband died from a wound
received in the Civil War.

She took a pair of mules and a wagon 120 miles
over the mountains and through enemy lines
during the winter of 1865 to pick up her husband's
remains and bring them back home to Monroe County
for burial.
